Goosebumps®
MOVIE NOVEL

Edited and introduced by R.L. Stine

Based on the
Screenplay by Darren Lemke
Story by Scott Alexander & Larry Karaszewski

SCHOLASTIC

Scholastic Children's Books
An imprint of Scholastic Ltd
Euston House, 24 Eversholt Street, London, NW1 1DB, UK
Registered office: Westfield Road, Southam, Warwickshire, CV47 0RA
SCHOLASTIC, GOOSEBUMPS, GOOSEBUMPS HORRORLAND and associated logos are trademarks
and/or registered trademarks of Scholastic Inc.

First Published in the US by Scholastic Inc, 2015
First published in the UK by Scholastic Ltd, 2016

ISBN 978 1407 15815 0

Goosebumps books created by Parachute Press, Inc.

A CIP catalogue record for this book
is available from the British Library.

Printed by CPI Group (UK) Ltd, Croydon, CR0 4YY
Papers used by Scholastic Children's Books are made
from wood grown in sustainable forests.

5 7 9 10 8 6 4

www.scholastic.co.uk

INTRODUCTION
R.L. STINE

I had a nightmare last night. I dreamed that I was writing the introduction to this book. Behind me, someone murmured the strange words that bring Slappy, the evil dummy, to life: *"Karru Marri Odonna Loma Molonu Karrano."*

I heard those frightening words in my dream, and I woke up shivering. I spun around, expecting the dummy with his cruel grin and cold stare to be standing there, ready to terrorize me. But . . . no sign of him.

Luckily, nightmares like that don't come true.

The next morning, I had some good news. I hurried to tell my wife, Jane. "Jack Black is going to play ME in the Goosebumps movie," I said. "Jack Black is hilarious!"

Jane nodded.

"He's wonderful. He's terrific! He'll be a great ME!" I exclaimed, thumping the breakfast table with my fist.

The dog looked up from her first nap of the day, wondering what the fuss was about.

"I wonder how he'll play me," I said, my mind spinning. "Sophisticated, maybe? Darkly mysterious? An evil genius?"

"Probably as a lunatic," Jane said. "Or is that too real?"

◊　　◊　　◊

A few weeks later, Jack flew in to New York City, where I live, and we had lunch. We had a good conversation and a lot of laughs.

"I know how I'm going to play you," Jack told me over dessert. "I'm going to play you as *you*—only a lot more sinister."

That sounded right to me. In person, I'm not very sinister. An Ohio newspaper once wrote: "In person, R.L. Stine is about as scary as an optometrist." I'm basically a jolly guy who likes to sit at a keyboard all day and write things to frighten children.

I was delighted that Jack Black would star in the Goosebumps movie. And just as delighted when the three teenagers in the story were cast. Dylan Minnette, Odeya Rush, and Ryan Lee were all seventeen and extremely talented and nice. I had a lot of fun talking with them on the set in Atlanta, where the movie was filmed.

◊ ◊ ◊

Since the movie was announced, everyone asks me this question: *Which book is the movie about?*

This was a difficult decision. And the question *had* to be answered before the movie could be written. Which story should the movie tell? Which evil character should star in the film?

Should it be one of the Slappy the Dummy books? *The Haunted Mask*? *Welcome to Horrorland*? One of the Monster

Blood tales? Dr. Maniac? Murder the Clown? Those nasty little lawn gnomes?

I've written more than 125 Goosebumps books. So choosing *one* of them for the film was a hard decision, to say the least.

Then the script-writing team had a brilliant idea: "Why should we base the movie on one book? Let's try to squeeze as many of the Goosebumps characters into the story as we can."

And that's just what happened.

The writers set up a major challenge for themselves: Use *dozens* of monsters and villains and crazy creatures from the Goosebumps books. Create a story in which R.L. Stine and the teenagers have to battle just about every bad-news character ever to appear.

Yes, all in one movie: the Abominable Snowman of Pasadena, the gigantic praying mantis from *A Shocker on Shock Street*, plus Slappy at his most cacklingest, zombies, staggering scarecrows, the Werewolf of Fever Swamp, and nasty lawn gnomes everywhere you look.

How will these creatures ever be defeated and sent back to where they came from? Well . . . that's what the film is all about.

This book tells the whole story. It has all the scares and all the laughs—and all the surprises and startling twists— you'll see in the movie. And you'll also find . . .

HEY! WAIT!

What are *you* doing here? Slappy! Get away! Get *out* of here! Nightmares don't come true! Slappy—please . . .

THANKS FOR THE WARM WELCOME, R.L. I'M HAPPY TO SEE YOU, TOO. YOU KNOW WHAT *R.L.* STANDS FOR, DON'T YOU? REAL LOSER. HA-HA-HA.

YOU'RE LOOKING GOOD, R.L. IS THAT YOUR NOSE, OR ARE YOU EATING A TOADSTOOL? I LIKE WHAT YOU DID WITH YOUR HAIR. AND NOTICE I SAID HAIR, NOT HAIRS! HA-HA-HA. YOU KNOW, I'VE SEEN BETTER SKIN ON AN ONION! HA-HA.

ACTUALLY, I'M KIDDING. I THINK YOU'RE PRETTY. PRETTY UGLY! HA-HA-HA.

DOES YOUR FACE HURT? IT'S KILLING ME! HA-HA-HA.

BUT ENOUGH POLITE CONVERSATION: I JUST CAME TO TELL EVERYONE WHO THE REAL STAR OF THE MOVIE IS. LET ME GIVE YOU ALL A HINT. IT'S NOT SPELLED *R.L.* HA-HA-HA.

ENJOY THIS BOOK, EVERYONE. I'M SURE YOU'LL LOVE FINDING OUT WHO THE REAL DUMMY IS!

HA-HA-HA-HA!

CHAPTER 1

I never believed we would *actually* move away from New York City. Not when my mom put her arm around me and said, "Zach, we need a fresh start." Not when she told me my aunt Lorraine lived in the perfect little town for us and had found her a great job. Not until we packed all our stuff into a U-Haul, hooked it up to the back of the station wagon, and drove away.

Can you blame me? I mean, who ditches New York City to go live in some tiny, dead-end, drop-dead-boring town in the middle of nowhere?

My mom, Gale Cooper, that's who.

And for some reason, she had to drag me along for the ride.

My mom promised me I'd love Madison as soon as I saw it. Here's what I saw as our car chugged across some rusty old bridge into town:

A sign reading WELCOME TO MADISON, POPULATION 28,245.

Translation: *Welcome to Nowheresville, Population YOU.*

A cutesy little downtown with about four buildings and the same number of people.

A strip of restaurants, including a noodle shop advertising "Sushi Wednesdays!" My stomach churned just thinking about what might pass for sushi here.

My mom was gazing through the windshield all starstruck, like we were driving straight through Times Square. "You know what I love about this place? No franchises. That's refreshing."

I slumped down in the passenger seat. "Did we go back in time when we crossed that bridge? Are we sure they have Wi-Fi?"

"No, Zach, families just sit around and listen to the radio by candlelight." My mom grinned.

Very funny, Mom.

"Are you positive there weren't any other places looking for vice principals?" I asked. "Maybe Guantanamo Bay? North Korea?"

She just laughed.

We pulled up to a red light, right beside a Madison Township cop car. The two cops inside were fast asleep. This was clearly the kind of town where nothing ever happened, or I might have started to worry.

◇ ◇ ◇

Our new house was . . . pretty much a typical house. Yard, picket fence, welcome mat. I groaned. This was going to feel like living inside a sitcom.

"Look, a yard!" my mom said. She's even better at fake enthusiasm than she is at bad jokes. They must teach it at vice principal school. "You'd never have something like this in New York!"

"Mom, you don't have to keep selling me on this place." I hoisted one of the boxes out of the trunk. "I'm staying. Because I love you—"

"Aww, honey, I love *you*."

"—and I looked into it," I added, grinning. "Legally, I can't live on my own until I'm eighteen."

She shook her head and went inside. I took a moment to look around, trying to bend my mind around it: *This is your life*.

There was a flicker of movement in the next-door neighbor's window. At least, I thought there was. But as soon as I turned to look, everything went still. There was no one there.

Great. Spying neighbors. One more thing to love about small-town life. In New York City, you were never really alone—but you got really good at ignoring everyone around you, and they got good at ignoring you. Just the way I liked it.

The inside of the house was pretty much what you'd expect from the outside. Sitcom-style suburban living.

"Look at this kitchen!" my mom said, spinning in circles around the huge room. "It's bigger than our old apartment."

She was right about that. It was huge. Every room in the house was huge compared to what I was used to.

Waste of space, if you ask me.

"We don't cook," I reminded her.

"But look at all this counter space to put the takeout on!" Then she paused, cocking her ear to one side. "Do you hear that?"

I listened hard. "Uh . . . I don't hear anything."

"Exactly."

I knew what she meant. In New York, you were never far from the noise of sirens, trucks backing up, construction drills, cars honking, drivers shouting, doors slamming— people *living*, and doing it basically right on top of you. In Madison, there was nothing but chirping birds and a soft whisper of wind.

So I got it. I just didn't understand why she *liked* it.

"Live, from New York . . ." a voice intoned behind me. I whirled around to see Aunt Lorraine, talking into her fist as if it were a microphone. ". . . it's my sister, Gale, with special guest, my nephew, Zach!"

"Hey, Aunt Lorraine." I wondered if she'd notice if I inched backward a little. Aunt Lorraine was a cheek-pincher. "Nice to see you."

"Gale, he gets more handsome every time I see him," she gushed. "So good-looking!"

"Thanks, Aunt Lorraine."

Just to be clear: I'm not handsome. The only people who think I am good-looking are related to me.

"Just a beautiful boy," she said. "And let's be honest, you were an ugly baby."

Uh . . . thanks?

"Lorraine . . ." My mom shook her head.

"It's fine," my aunt insisted. "He's handsome now, and it's not like he's gonna go back to being ugly. Handsome isn't a phase. No one goes ugly, handsome, then back to ugly. The danger's passed." She looked into the distance for a moment, and I could tell—from the way she wrinkled her nose—that she was remembering my baby pictures. "What an *ugly* baby."

"Yes, Aunt Lorraine, you bring that up every time you see me."

"Ooh, I almost forgot!" She rifled through her shopping bag and pulled out a Yankees cap. A bedazzled Yankees cap, glistening with the sparkle of a million plastic rhinestones. "From my new signature men's line!"

She slipped it onto my head.

"Very . . . thoughtful," my mom said. I could tell she was trying to not laugh. She gestured at me. "Say thank you."

There were a whole lot of things I wanted to say about that hat. *Thank you* wasn't high on the list.

"It's a limited edition," Aunt Lorraine said proudly. "You won't see a lot of men wearing that hat."

"I can't imagine I'll see anyone wearing it," I mumbled. "I'm, uh, going to go unload the car now."

I got out of there fast, leaving my mother and her sister to catch up. Maybe talk some more about how handsome I was these days. Especially in my sparkly new cap.

I managed to stack about three boxes and make it halfway back up the driveway when I felt the bottom of the first box start to give way. *Uh-oh.* I snaked a hand underneath to prop it up, but that tilted the stack too far, and the top box started to slip, and then the whole stack teetered—

And then I was standing amidst a heap of dented cardboard boxes. One of which busted open, spilling out a mountain of boxer shorts.

Which was, of course, the perfect moment for the world's most beautiful girl to poke her head out of the window next door and say hi.

CHAPTER 2

"So you're the new neighbor," the girl said, eyes not on me but on the boxer shorts.

She was . . . wow. She had this long brown hair, all thick and wavy like from a shampoo commercial. And these bright blue eyes, the kind that made you want to write poems about the sky and the ocean and all that junk. If I were the kind of guy who wrote poems. Which, obviously, I am not.

"Nice to meet you," I said, frantically piling my underwear back into the box.

"How long was the drive from New York?"

How did she know I was from New York?

"I could tell from your pretty hat," she explained.

Oh. Right. The hat. The bedazzled, pink and purple, tackiness-hall-of-fame hat. I wanted to evaporate, right on the spot. Actually, I wanted the *hat* to evaporate. Or spontaneously combust. When that didn't happen, I whipped it off my head and shoved it into my back pocket. "This was actually a gift from my aunt."

The girl had a smile like a cat. "It's also a gift for me and

everyone else who gets to see you wearing it."

Play it cool, I reminded myself . . . like I had ever, in my life, been cool. "Then you are welcome, girl-in-the-window. I'm Zach, by the way."

"I'm Hannah." She looked over her shoulder then, all quick and nervous. "I gotta go."

Just like that, she was gone. And in her place? A middle-aged creeper with thick black glasses and a tight-fitting black suit. He looked kind of like a professor . . . if there were such a thing as a professor of weird.

"Hi. We're just moving in," I said, figuring that was the kind of neighborly thing you said out in the sitcom suburbs.

The guy just stared at me, no expression whatsoever. It was like his face was made out of wax.

"Just me and my mom," I added, then indicated the hat, in case that was throwing him off. "This hat was a gift."

Maybe the guy couldn't talk? Or maybe this was like one of those creepy movies where the weird guy next door is a serial killer?

Professor Weird raised an arm and pointed. "See that fence?"

"Uh, yup?" Tough not to see it: black, high, wrought iron, running straight down the border between our houses.

"Stay on your side of it," he said. "Stay away from my daughter, stay away from me, and we won't have any problems." He slammed the window shut and pulled down the blinds. I could hear him turning what sounded like a lock.

A big lock.

And they say *New Yorkers* aren't friendly!

CHAPTER 3

I got the boxes together again and headed back inside. Mom and Aunt Lorraine were already unpacking. I guess we really did live there now. "Just met our neighbor," I told them. "What a sweet teddy bear."

"Mr. Shivers?" Lorraine brightened. "He moved to town a few years ago. Very mysterious, very sexy. I love his scent. It's like this sensuous, sweaty pine tree."

"Not my type," I told her, shuddering. Aunt Lorraine is great and all, but when she starts talking about *sensuous pine trees*, I kind of want to stick my finger down my throat and gag for a while.

My mom ripped off the packing tape on another box and opened it up. She pulled out a wooden plaque that'd been sitting on top, and we all fell silent.

Mom swallowed. "Oh."

It was a big, fancy plaque, with NEW YORK FIRE DEPARTMENT MEMORIAL spelled out in big, fancy letters.

I hated the sight of it.

"You okay, sweetheart?" she asked in That Voice, the

wobbly one that said: *I can keep it together, but only if you can.*

"Yeah, sorry." I cleared my throat and made my face a total blank. I could hold it together for her, keep her from worrying about me. My dad would have wanted it that way. "I'm gonna go to my room and unpack. Knock it off my bucket list."

I got out of there before either of them could say anything that might make one of us cry. I hated crying.

Plus, I'd done enough of that lately.

See, here's the thing about my mom and me. We're doing a pretty good job of being just the two of us. But we both know that's not the way it's supposed to be. It's supposed to be *the three of us.* Me, my mom, and my dad.

Once I was safe in my new room, door shut behind me, I cued up the video on my dad's old camcorder. The video I've watched more times than I would ever admit. There was my dad, all dressed up in uniform, getting a medal from the mayor.

I was so proud of him that day. I wanted to climb up on the roof and shout it to the whole world: *That's my dad.*

I'd watched the video so many times, I knew the mayor's speech by heart:

"We have forgotten what the word *hero* means. It's not about throwing the winning pass or being on the cover of a magazine. A true hero is someone who gives of themselves, who sacrifices, who throws themselves in harm's

11

way to protect others. Lieutenant Neal Cooper is one of those heroes."

Sometimes I worried I would never be able to live up to that, never be the kind of hero my dad was.

Sometimes, though, I wished he hadn't been quite so eager to throw himself in harm's way for someone else. Maybe if he hadn't been such a good hero, he would still be here for us.

My mom swung the door open, and I quickly shut off the video. There was no reason for her to know how often I watched it. That would just make her worry, and these days, my mom worried enough.

"You okay, honey?"

"Just found some old baby pictures," I told her, trying to sound cheerful. "I really did look like baby King Kong."

She bought it. I could tell from how the fake, tense smile on her face turned into a real one.

That's when I decided I really would try to make this whole move-to-nowhere thing work. For her. Now that my dad wasn't around, it was up to me to make some sacrifices of my own.

CHAPTER 4

Of course, there's making sacrifices . . . and then there's starting a new school in the middle of the year with your mom as your vice principal.

Which was more like sacrificing yourself into an active volcano.

She drove us to school the next morning and pulled into her faculty parking spot. "All right! Let's go make friends!"

She sounded like an overcaffeinated cheerleader. My mom is a morning person. It's incredibly annoying.

I locked the doors before she could get out. "What do you think you're doing?"

"Going to work," she said. "Do some educatin', some administratin'!"

See what I mean about the perky?

Maybe it was time to lay down some ground rules. "Mom. I'm the new kid, which presents its own set of obstacles. Not sure walking in with the vice principal is the play."

"Don't be ridiculous, I'm not just the vice principal. I'm also your mom."

What is it about parents and their inability to grasp the most basic facts of life?

She unlocked the doors; I locked them again.

"Tell you what," I proposed. "Give me a sixty-second head start, so I at least have a chance."

"Deal," she said. Then, more seriously, "Promise you'll give it a shot."

I sighed. "You know I can't promise you that."

This time, she was the one who locked me in.

"I promise," I said, accepting defeat. "And this door-locking thing, come on. You're better than that."

I winked at her, then jumped out of the car and headed toward school. I had sixty seconds to put as much distance between me and the vice principal as I could, and I wasn't wasting a single one.

The school was pretty much like any other school, or at least, like every school I'd ever been to. I mean, the campus was a lot bigger than I was used to, but the kids looked about the same. You know, the usual: artsy kids, preppies, nerds, jocks.

The day ended with an assembly to introduce the new vice principal. I was waiting for it to start when a skinny kid with a bucktoothed grin dropped into the seat next to me.

"Hi, I'm Champ," he said. "So, how are you liking Madison so far?"

"It's everything I hoped and more," I told him.

Onstage, the principal stepped up to the mic, talking straight through the screeching feedback. "All right, settle down. I'm pleased to introduce our new vice principal, Ms. Cooper. I hope you show her the same respect you show me."

Judging from the fart sounds coming from the back row, I was guessing all that respect didn't add up to much.

"Who did that?" shouted Principal Garrison, squinting into the audience. "Who did that?!"

Shockingly, no one raised a hand.

My mom stepped forward to the microphone. The football coach applauded wildly, but as for everyone else? Dead silence.

"Hey, everyone," she said, not sounding nervous at all. I was proud of her up there—but I couldn't help wishing she was up onstage at any other school but this one. "I know I speak for the entire administration when I say we're all excited for tomorrow's Fall Dance. I can't wait to get jiggly with it."

Seriously, *any* other school.

Champ leaned toward me. "She's worse than the last one," he whispered.

I glared at him. "That's my mom."

"And the last one was *excellent*," he added quickly.

"And, as a final reminder, be safe and have fun," my mom said.

"You going to the dance with anyone?" Champ asked

me. Like I didn't have *does not do dances* written all over me?

"No."

"Cool. Neither am I," he said, totally not getting it. "Maybe we should go together."

"Uh, together?"

"Not 'together' together," he said quickly. "Not, like, dancing together—although we could get the crowd into it and then we each split off with different girls. Yeah, it could work a bunch of different ways." He handed me a business card. "Here. Give me a call or text me or tweet me. This card has all my contact info." He pointed to the tiny print. "This is my home address, and that's my locker number."

"Thank you, I guess?"

And just like that, I had officially made my first Madison High School friend.

Way to go, Zach.

CHAPTER 5

Even in the sitcom suburbs, someone had to take out the garbage. And just like back in the city, that someone was me. I tugged the bags around the back of the house and stuffed them into the garbage cans. It got really dark out there at night, and I still wasn't used to it. I wasn't used to the quiet, either. Nothing but chirping crickets and the rustle of grass.

It was all too easy to imagine someone out there in the darkness, hiding. Watching. Waiting.

Actually, it was kind of easy to imagine I wasn't imagining it. "Hello?" I said, feeling kind of stupid. But I just had that feeling. That feeling you get when you're being watched.

I lifted the garbage can lid and held it in front of me like a shield. A lame, plastic shield that reeked of garbage, maybe, but you use what you got. "Someone there?" I said into the night, hoping I sounded tough.

Behind me, a branch snapped. I spun around, ducking behind the garbage lid. I peeked out from it just enough to see a shadowy figure watching me.

It was Hannah, the girl next door, waving at me from

her side of the fence. "Did I scare you?" she teased.

"*Pfft.* No." Then I realized I was still holding the garbage can lid.

"Because you jumped, like, ten feet in the air."

"I, uh, jump a lot. That's how I stay in such great shape." I decided it was probably time to change the subject before she took a closer look at my muscles. (Or lack thereof.) "Didn't see you at school today."

She smiled that cat smile of hers. "Why? Were you looking?"

"No, I just—"

"I'm homeschooled."

"Oh, by your dad?" I didn't know what to say about that. Stuck in a room all day, every day, with Professor Creepy? "He seems . . . nice," I said. "Intense. And a little tense."

I was trying to be polite, but she looked like she knew what I was getting at. "Don't take it personally. He doesn't like anybody."

"I totally misread that," I joked. "I thought we had a good connection. So . . ." I wracked my brain, trying to think of something fascinating to say. I didn't want her to go back inside yet. "Is there anything fun to do around here? Aside from Sushi Wednesdays, obviously?"

Not exactly fascinating, but it did the trick.

"I'm the wrong person to ask," she admitted. "It's just me and my dad, and I don't like to leave him alone."

"Come on," I pressed. "There's got to be *something* fun you do, aside from scaring your neighbors."

"Well . . ." She paused for a second, like she was trying to decide whether or not I could be trusted. "There is one thing I like to do." She nodded toward the street. "Come on."

CHAPTER 6

Hannah wouldn't tell me where we were going, but I followed her anyway. Down the block, around the corner, and down an extremely unlit street that dead-ended in an overgrown grove of trees.

"Are you taking me somewhere to kill me?" I joked. Well, mostly joked. "I'm just curious."

"I'm playing it by ear." She slipped behind a tree and disappeared into the shadows. Leaving me alone in the empty night.

"Yes, Zach, follow the stranger into the woods," I muttered. Then I followed the stranger into the woods.

I followed her through the trees, and I followed her as she slid beneath a rusty old fence. Then I gasped when I saw what lay on the other side.

It was an amusement park.

Hannah flipped some kind of power switch hidden in the dirt, and the place lit up like . . . well, like an amusement park. A lot of the bulbs were burned out, and the ones that were left flickered and strobed, but there was enough light

to see the place. The rides were creaky and rusted over, but you could tell that once, a long time ago, this park had been something amazing.

"They started building it years ago, but they ran out of money," Hannah explained. "So now it just sits there."

A whole amusement park that no one had ever used? It felt like a violation of some law of nature. All those rides, just waiting to be ridden. All those fun-house rooms, echoing with the laughter of invisible children.

I shivered, feeling a sudden chill down my spine.

Hannah hopped a rusty turnstile and headed straight for a Ferris wheel that was missing half its spokes. Then she started to climb.

"I come here all the time," she called down to me. "What are you afraid of?"

"I'm not afraid," I insisted. "I'm, uh, just not current with my tetanus shot." The Ferris wheel was studded with rusty nails and bolts. You could probably get tetanus just from looking at it.

Hannah was already halfway to the top.

"So? What's a little gangrene?" I muttered. Then I followed her up.

It wasn't such a hard climb, but it was a long one, and my arms were aching by the time we made it to the top. But it was worth it all for the view. The whole town was spread out beneath us like a bunch of dollhouses twinkling with lights.

From up there, it almost looked like civilization.

"You can see everything from up here," I said in awe. I could see why Hannah loved it. Up there so close to the sky, the quiet didn't bother me as much. And I had to admit, there was one good thing about being out in the middle of nowhere: You could see the stars.

I'd almost forgotten what that was like, to look up at a sky sparkling with the light of all those faraway suns. I wished I could stay up there forever.

"So, why'd you move to Madison?" Hannah asked.

"My mom said to me, 'Zach, if you could go anywhere in the world, where would it be?' And I said, 'Can we *please* move to Madison, Delaware? That's my dream.'"

She didn't smile. "Are you always this sarcastic?"

"Always? Not always." I thought about it. "Usually."

I don't know if it was the place or the girl, but something about that night made it seem okay to tell the truth. Not just okay—necessary. "It's just been my mom and me since my dad died last year," I admitted. "So . . . yeah."

"Sorry," she said, and I got the feeling she understood everything I was saying and everything I wasn't saying. Like how it was easier to be sarcastic than to be real, because being real meant saying things that hurt. How not feeling anything was easier than feeling *something*, when that something was so huge and so sad.

"I don't really think about it much anymore." That was a

lie, but I think she knew that. We both just pretended to believe it. "What about you?"

"I never knew my mom," she said. "And my dad and I are always moving from one town to the next."

"That really sucks."

We sat there together for a while without talking, but it was the good kind of quiet, the kind where you know you're both thinking about the same thing. It felt good, not having to explain myself or pretend things were okay when they weren't. But it couldn't last forever.

"Hannah, can I ask you something?" I said finally.

She nodded.

"How do we get down?"

She laughed, and showed me the best way to shimmy down the spokes. Somehow, we both managed not to plummet to our deaths. And when my feet were safely back on solid ground, I managed not to kneel down and kiss the dirt. (Although I was tempted.)

I would never have been able to find my way back home in the dark, but Hannah knew exactly where to go.

"Thanks for tonight," I told her as we reached the fence that separated our houses. "It was the least terrible time I've had here."

She clasped her hand over her heart. *"Awwwww."*

Then she waved good-night and turned to go inside. I had no idea if I'd ever even get to talk to her again. If it was any

other girl, I might have tried to psych myself up to ask her out on a date. But Hannah didn't really seem like the dinner-and-a-movie type. Which was a good thing, because neither was I.

"Hey, Hannah," I said, thinking fast. "I'm probably gonna take out the trash on Tuesdays and Thursdays, so if you feel like creeping up on someone, that works for me."

"I'll keep that in mind, Scaredy-Cat." She smiled.

I smiled.

I think we were about to have A Moment when a hand reached out of the darkness and seized her shoulder.

Hannah gasped. I nearly screamed.

Then her father's face peered out of the shadows.

"Where were you?" he snapped.

"I'm sorry." In a heartbeat, she'd transformed into a completely different person, meek and terrified.

Mr. Shivers was practically shaking with rage. "Get. In. The. House. *Now.*"

Her head dropped. She slunk up the driveway, looking just about as defeated as anyone I've ever seen. *What kind of a dad treats his daughter like that?* That's what I wanted to say—in fact, there were a *lot* of things I wanted to say. But then Shivers fixed his glare of fury on me, and I lost my voice.

"This is the last time I'm warning you." He wasn't shouting anymore, and somehow, that was even scarier. The guy was like a nuclear bomb, just waiting to go off. "If you don't stay away from us, something *very bad* will happen."

"I believe you," I said, and I did. This guy was beyond

creepy.

This guy was dangerous.

I was a little afraid to turn my back on him . . . but I was even more afraid that if I kept standing there, he might set me on fire with his eyes.

So I ran into the house, and I didn't stop running until I'd made it up the stairs and into my room. I slammed the door behind me, finally safe.

For now.

CHAPTER 7

The next night, the wind rattled against the windows. I tried to tune it out. This was no time to be creeped out by middle-of-nowhere night noises—I had math homework to do.

"What is X?" I murmured to myself, skimming my pencil tip across the word problem. "Wait, *where* is X?"

Then there was a noise I couldn't tune out.

A scream.

A loud blood-curdling, horror-movie-style, someone's-murdering-me-right-now-with-a-gigantic-knife scream.

And it sounded like Hannah.

I bounded to the window. In the house next door, shadows flickered behind the closed curtains. I couldn't make out any shapes, but it must have been Hannah and her dad.

There were more noises: Glass breaking. Wood snapping. And then . . .

Nothing.

The Shiverses' house went totally dark—and totally silent.

"Hannah!" I cried, and ran downstairs. I flung myself

through our front door, climbed over the fence, and pounded on Hannah's door until it swung open.

Mr. Shivers stood in the doorway, glaring down at me. "What."

I was panting.

I was terrified.

"I heard a scream. Is Hannah okay?"

"There was no scream," he said flatly. "You didn't hear anything. Now, get out of here, or the last scream you'll ever hear will be yours."

The door slammed shut in my face.

The guy was unbelievable. And unbelievably creepy.

I knew he'd done something to Hannah. I had to do something to help. I ran back to our house, heading straight for the kitchen.

My mom looked up from her computer like nothing was wrong. She pulled off her headphones. "Hey, sweetie, how do you feel about quinoa for dinner?"

"Mom! Hannah's in trouble!" I didn't have time to explain. I grabbed the phone from the table and dialed 911.

My mom looked clueless. "Who's Hannah?"

It took the operator forever to pick up.

My mom grabbed my shoulders. "Zach, you're scaring me. What is going on?"

I explained it to the 911 operator—then I explained it to my mom. We sat there together, waiting for the sound of sirens.

Finally, a cop car came screaming down the street, turning into Shivers's driveway. I ran out to join it, my mom hot on my heels. I knew she'd want me to stay safely on the sidelines.

Absolutely. No. Way.

There were two cops, and they marched up to Shivers's door like they meant business. This time, he opened it on the first knock.

"You're under arrest!" the guy cop said.

His partner put a hand on his arm. "Whoa, whoa. Love the enthusiasm, but we're not there yet." She turned to Shivers. "I'm Officer Stevens, this is training Officer Brooks."

"Sorry about that," Officer Brooks said.

I couldn't believe they were being so polite. Or so slow! I was about to crawl out of my skin. When were they going to get inside and find Hannah?

"We got a call about a possible ten-sixteen at your residence," Stevens said, "which is . . ." She turned to Brooks, waiting for him to fill in the answer.

"A domestic disturbance," he said eagerly. Wait, was he *flirting* with her?

She beamed, practically batting her eyelashes. "You are such a fast learner."

Shivers looked as disgusted as I felt. "What do you mean, domestic disturbance?"

"Do you want to take this one, Brooks?" Stevens offered.

"A domestic disturbance is . . . it's like a . . . it's domes-

tic, so it's inside the house, and, uh . . ."

"Exactly, yes." Officer Stevens nodded sharply. "And I would just add to that, it's basically anything going wrong inside your house. On a domestic basis."

I wanted to shake them both. Even more, I wanted to push them aside, shove Shivers out of the way, and go find Hannah for myself. But they were cops, Shivers was a grown-up, and as far as they were concerned, I was just a kid.

So I stood there with my mouth shut, waiting.

Sometimes, being *just a kid* stinks.

"*Hmm,*" Shivers said, playing nice for the cops. He took a moment to pretend he was actually thinking about it. "I've been alone here all night. Haven't heard a thing."

I couldn't keep quiet anymore, not after that. "He's lying! Where's Hannah? I know it was Hannah screaming."

Shivers smiled at the cops—or at least, he tried to smile. It was even creepier than his normal expression. "Happy" didn't really suit him.

"Hannah is my daughter," he said. "She was staying with me for a while until her mother sorted a few things out with her new husband. She went back to London yesterday afternoon."

It was a lie. I knew it was a lie, because Hannah had told me she'd never even *met* her mother. So the question was, why was he lying?

And what had he done with her?

CHAPTER 8

Behind Shivers, a woman's scream echoed.

That was all it took to get Brooks and Stevens inside. Finally!

My mom and I chased after the officers, following the sound of the screams—all the way to the big-screen TV, where a woman was screaming in black-and-white while some cheesy old-school monster chased after her.

Shivers muted it with his remote. "Surround sound," he said smugly. "I didn't know it was a crime."

Officer Brooks's eyes widened. "I've seen this movie. The girl turns out to be a monster, too."

"Spoiler alert," his partner said, rolling her eyes. "You just ruined it for everyone."

Brooks shrugged. "Sorry. Rookie mistake."

My mom stepped in front of them and extended her hand to Shivers. I couldn't believe it. My own *mother*, shaking hands with this guy like he hadn't just done something terrible and then lied to our faces about it!

"I'm so sorry," she said. "I'm Gale Cooper, your new

neighbor. Beautiful home."

"A pleasure," Shivers said. He almost sounded like he meant it. "Thank you so much for stopping by—and bringing your delightful son. And the police."

"Again, I'm so sorry."

It galled me the way she kept apologizing like I was the one who'd done something wrong.

There *was* something wrong, all right, but it was Shivers. Why couldn't the rest of them see it? He was breathing too fast and fidgeting like he couldn't wait to get us out of his house. Like he had something to hide.

"Hannah!" I shouted.

Shivers glanced toward the stairs. It was subtle, and fast, but I saw it.

"Hannah!" I ran for the stairs—or tried to. The cops grabbed my arms and held me back.

"Whoa there, big guy," Stevens said.

"Should I tase him?" Brooks asked eagerly. "Let me tase him."

"Love your moxie," Stevens said, "but let's hold off."

So they didn't tase me, but they did muscle me out of the house.

"Do you know what the punishment is for filing a fake police report?" Stevens asked me.

"Three years?" Brooks guessed.

"Close. It's actually just a written warning."

I ignored them. "Mom, tell me you don't believe him! Surround sound? *Seriously?*"

"Zach, enough!" It was her I-mean-business voice. "We're going home."

She was the mom, and I was the kid, right? So that's what we did. We went home.

I paced around the kitchen like a caged animal. "Mom, Hannah's in trouble, I *know* it."

She shook her head. "I know what you're doing, Zach. I'm not an idiot. We're not leaving because you are afraid of our neighbor. You know that, right? You need to accept that this is our home now."

She had it all wrong. Except she was a little bit right, too. And suddenly that little bit grew into a great big angry bit, and I couldn't keep it inside anymore. "No, it's not *my* home," I snapped.

"Zach—"

"I've tried, Mom. But I don't want to be here. You didn't even *ask* me if I wanted to move."

"Zach, we had to leave New York."

"No!" I shouted. "*You* did."

The truth landed like a giant boulder, smashing us both. She didn't say anything, and I didn't have anything left to say.

I shut myself up in my bedroom. A few minutes later, I heard the front door close.

She was gone.

CHAPTER 9

Aunt Lorraine came over to baby-sit me while my mother was chaperoning the dance. Like I needed a baby-sitter—I am *sixteen* years old! But there was nothing I could do about it, just like there was nothing I could do about Hannah being stuck in that house with a madman, and there was nothing I could do about being stuck in this town, hundreds of miles from my real life.

It wasn't Aunt Lorraine's fault, though, so I tried my best to be nice. I even sat there with her while she bedazzled a pair of jeans with sequins and told me about her love life. It's not like I had anything better to do.

Even pretending to pay attention was hard, though.

". . . so, we went out to Sushi Wednesday, both of us had the chicken teriyaki, which was sensational, and then I haven't heard from him since, not that I even really care . . ."

As she droned on and on, I couldn't stop thinking about Hannah. I was thinking about her so much, in fact, that when I saw her shadow in Shivers's upstairs window, I thought I was imagining it.

I blinked, hard.

No, not my imagination: real. That was Shivers's silhouette against the curtain, with Hannah right beside him. She hadn't gone to London—she was right here. And she was in trouble.

I knew it.

"So, do you think he's playing hard to get?" Aunt Lorraine asked. "Or, the more likely scenario, he lost his phone?"

I barely heard her. "I think he lost his phone," I repeated. "You know, Aunt Lorraine, I totally forgot, but I have a huge test tomorrow, so I'm just gonna be studying for the rest of the night." I backed toward the stairs, hoping to make it up to my room before she could start asking questions or poke holes in my story. "So, definitely don't come in, okay? See ya."

She bought it. "'Night, sweetie!"

As soon as I made it upstairs, I made a quick phone call. Then I dug up my old flashlight. And quietly as I could, I eased open the window and climbed through it.

CHAPTER 10

I wasn't alone outside for long. Champ came wandering up our driveway, wearing a suit that looked like it belonged to someone's dead grandfather.

"*Psst,*" I whispered, loud as I could from my perch beside Shivers's fence. "Over here!"

Champ changed course and headed toward me. "Wait, where are the girls?" he asked. "Is *that* what you're wearing to the dance?" He was obviously confused, and I couldn't blame him. It's possible I hadn't been precisely, absolutely honest with him when I'd called.

"Get down," I hissed.

He looked at me like I was nuts. "No way! This is a new suit. Where are the girls?"

"Yeah, about that . . . I just said that to get you over here," I admitted. "I need your help."

His face fell. "So, there are no girls?"

"Well, there is one girl . . ."

"Okay!" He held up a hand for a high five. "My man!"

". . . but she's locked in the house and her dad's a

psychopath."

Champ considered this for a moment. Then he shrugged. "Does she have a friend?"

"I'm serious," I said. "And since the police don't believe me, we need to break into this house and get her out."

Even I could hear how crazy it sounded.

"You know, you *said* there'd be girls," Champ complained. "Not only are there no girls, there's a psychopath. And I'm in a suit—"

"You look very nice," I told him. A little sucking up never hurt anyone.

"Thank you. But this is really not how I saw my night going. If we're gonna be friends, no more lying about girls!"

I nodded. *Deal.*

Before we could shake on it, the front door swung open. Shivers stepped out.

I yanked Champ down into the bushes with me.

"It's wet grass!" he hissed.

We crouched in the dew, watching Shivers climb into his car and squeal out of the driveway.

This was our chance: It was now or never.

I took a deep breath. "Let's go!"

While I was waiting for Champ to show up, I'd scoped out the grounds. Did a little reconnaissance, like they say in the movies. I'd decided there was no way we could bust through the front door. It was thick, steel reinforced, with at

least four locks. No, our best bet was the cellar on the side of the house. There were two giant wooden doors embedded in the ground, held together with a rusty old padlock. And I knew what to do with a padlock.

I gave it a light tug, just in case. Some people are forgetful about their locks.

Not Shivers.

"Well, we tried," Champ said hopefully. "Let's go to the dance."

I shook my head. Then I rifled through my pockets till I came up with a paper clip. After snapping it in half, I threaded both pieces into the lock.

Champ laughed. "That's not gonna work."

I ignored him. It was all a matter of feel. If I could find the right pin positions, hold them down while I spun the lock with the other wire, then maybe, just maybe—

Yessss. The lock popped open.

So did Champ's eyes. "Whoa," he breathed. "Where'd you learn to do that? New York?"

"YouTube."

Opening the cellar had been the easy part. Now we actually had to climb down inside. Into the darkness, deep down beneath the earth. Who knew what a guy like Shivers might be hiding in his cellar? I decided to give Champ a break.

"Stay here and watch the driveway," I suggested.

"Wait here? By *myself*?" His voice broke on the last word.

"Out in the *dark*?"

"Yeah, you're the lookout. If Shivers comes back, just give me a sign." I cupped my hands over my mouth and gave him my best imitation birdcall. *"Ha-hooo! Ha-hooo!"*

Champ nodded solemnly.

I had to admit, I felt a little better knowing a friend had my back. At least until he spoke: "Just so we're clear, if I sense danger, I will run the other way."

CHAPTER 11

Hannah's waiting, I reminded myself.

Then I turned on the flashlight and lowered myself into the pitch-black cellar, trying not to think about what else might be waiting down there for me.

Down in the cellar, the air was thick with dust and cobwebs, and every once in a while the flashlight beam caught a spider scuttling past.

It's no different from the subway, I told myself. *Nothing scary about being underground. Nothing to worry about at all . . .*

"*Yaiiii!*" I shrieked, as a fluttering black missile shot past my head, uttering a terrifying cry.

My heart pounding, I swiveled the flashlight beam toward the creature. "Whoa." I sighed with relief. Just a bird, and not even a real one.

A wooden cuckoo, popped out of a cuckoo clock. As I watched, it receded back into its nest of gears and clockwork.

I took a deep breath and waited for my heart to stop beating against my chest. Then I moved the flashlight away

from the clock and scanned the room.

"*Ohhhh.*" I froze with one foot in midair. The floor was littered with giant metal traps, their jagged teeth wider than my hand. I'd seen plenty of mousetraps in my time. But *no way* were these traps designed to catch anything the size of a mouse. Or even a rat. No, these had to be *bear* traps.

What kind of a lunatic covers his cellar floor with bear traps?

Was it the kind of lunatic who had a pet bear?

What had I gotten myself into?

I was seriously thinking about getting out of there—when a hand reached out of the darkness and clamped down on my shoulder. I stifled a scream and whirled around.

There was Champ, grinning at me in the darkness.

"What the heck, man?" No way was I letting him know how happy I was to see him. "Hey. You're supposed to be the lookout."

"And that's not going to change," he said. "I'll just be the lookout in here."

"By definition, you have to be somewhere out looking," I said. It was kind of useful having such a scaredy-cat around—it gave me a good excuse to act tough.

Champ didn't seem to care if he looked tough or not. "Let me explain something to you, Zacharias. You know how they say teenagers have no fear of death, that they'll never get hurt? Not me." He sounded almost proud. "I was born with the gift of fear. I remember being four and being

40

pushed on a swing and thinking, *This is how it ends*."

That explained a *lot*.

"You're not going to die," I promised him. "At least, not today."

"You're right, I'm being crazy—" Then he noticed the sharp metal teeth scattered across the floor. "Oh . . . bear traps."

Somewhere above us, there was a noise. Someone was up there.

"Let's go," I said.

"I agree."

I was already halfway up the stairs to the first floor before I realized Champ was scrambling in the opposite direction.

"I'm going back outside," he said. "I mean, like, somewhere without bear traps."

I didn't bother trying to talk him into following me. After all, this wasn't his fight. But I was maybe just a tiny, secret bit relieved when he changed his mind and decided he was better off following me. Even if he did manage to have two spider-web-related hissy fits by the time he made it to the top of the stairs.

The house was dark. But it wasn't empty. Up on the second floor, a floorboard creaked.

"Up there," I whispered, nodding at the ornate staircase. "Hannah?" I said it as loudly as I dared. (Which, admittedly, wasn't very loud.)

No answer. So we started to climb.

Shadows reached for us with long, dark tendrils. The steps creaked beneath our feet—which meant whoever was upstairs would know we were coming.

The darkness felt heavy. Oppressive. Behind me, I could hear Champ's teeth chattering, and I could feel the hair rising on the back of my neck. We were closing in.

But on what?

I stopped at one end of a long, narrow hallway. At the far end were two double doors, light seeping from the crack beneath them. The creaking noises were definitely coming from there.

I glanced over my shoulder at Champ. His face was a pale moon in the darkness. He shook his head, hard, message pretty clear: *No way. Not going in there.*

I nodded. *Oh, yes, we are.*

The doors opened easily into some kind of study. It was crowded with thick wooden shelves and a giant desk.

I skidded the flashlight beam over the shelves—and really wished I hadn't. A row of shrunken heads stared back at me with hollow eyes. *Was that what happened to the last guys foolish enough to break into Shivers's house?*

Champ reached for the desk lamp and tugged on its chain. The room lit with a warm orange glow. Which didn't make it any less creepy, because now we could see everything piled on the shelves—not just withered heads, but tribal masks with terrifying expressions, a giant gold sarcophagus, and a bunch of lumpy, homemade figures with pins sticking out of them.

"Please tell me those aren't *voodoo* dolls," Champ whispered, shuddering.

A second set of shelves was stacked full of thick, leather-bound manuscripts—each of them bound with a shiny brass lock. It wasn't any weirder than the bear traps or the shriveled heads. But there was something about those manuscripts that I didn't like. Something that gave me a bad feeling.

Maybe it was the fact that the locks were rattling.

On their own.

Champ didn't seem to notice anything. He'd already pulled a couple manuscripts off the shelf. "Whoa, check this out," he said. "*The Scarecrow Walks at Midnight. The Ghost Next Door. Night of the Living Dummy!*"

I'd never heard him sound so excited.

Champ gazed at the books in awe. "These are Goosebumps manuscripts," he said in a hushed voice.

"You mean, those kids' books?"

Champ looked at me like I'd suggested the earth was flat. "No way. *Kids'* books help you fall asleep," he corrected me. "*These* books keep you up all night." He turned a manuscript on its side and examined the author's name on the spine. "R.L. Stine. Man, whatever happened to that guy?"

That rang another bell. I felt like I'd heard some story a long time ago, but I couldn't bother thinking about some old guy who wrote books for little kids a million years ago.

"Who knows?" I said. "He just disappeared one day. Does it matter? Let's go."

But Champ wasn't going anywhere. "*The Abominable Snowman of Pasadena.*" He shook his head in wonder. "My grandmother lived in Pasadena. I stopped visiting her after reading this book."

"We're not here for a book club," I reminded him. I didn't know why he was making such a fuss. They were just *books*. How scary could they be?

He tugged at the book, trying to open it, but it was locked up tight like all the rest of them. "Why do you think they're locked?" he asked. "Can you pick it?"

I could have, but I didn't have to—there was a bright gold key sitting on the bottom shelf. I stuck it in the lock: perfect fit. The key turned, the lock popped free. "Mystery solved." I took the book out of his hands, set it back on the shelf, then flicked out the lights and headed for the door. "Now, let's get back to why we're—"

A shadowy figure materialized right behind Champ.

"Get down!" I shouted.

CHAPTER 12

I pushed Champ out of the way just as the shadow swung a baseball bat at his head. The bat whooshed through the space where he'd been a second before.

Then our enemy spoke.

"Zach?"

I flipped on the light. "Hannah?!"

She didn't look particularly happy to see us. "What are you doing in my house?"

"I, uh, thought you were chained up? Possibly?"

"Why would you think that?" She tried to sweep both of us into the hallway.

Was she serious? *Why* would I think she was in trouble? "Have you met your father?" I asked her.

Champ ignored the conversation and stuck out his hand for her to shake. She declined.

"I'm Champ, by the way," he said cheerfully. "We're going to the semiformal, if you want to come, and invite a friend . . . I don't care what she looks like."

But Hannah obviously wasn't listening. She was looking

past him, eyes fixed on the manuscript I'd unlocked.

"Did you . . ." She swallowed, hard. "Did you open that lock?"

"I may have," I admitted. "I'll just put it back and we'll pretend this whole thing never happened."

I reached around her and grabbed the manuscript. I just meant to slide it back into place, I really did. I didn't mean to open it.

It just happened.

"No!" Hannah cried. "Don't open it!"

Before I could ask her what the big deal was, a gale-force wind blasted us off our feet. "*Nooooo!*" I uttered a scream as we toppled backward into the wall.

Had I hit my head? Suddenly, I was seeing things.

I *must* have been seeing things, because surely there wasn't a fifteen-foot-tall, two-ton, hairy, fanged *monster* standing in the middle of the study.

Right?

"Nobody move," Hannah whispered, staring at the monster. Which meant she saw it, too. Which meant it was real.

Champ opened his mouth to scream, but no sound came out.

The monster's deafening roar made the floor tremble beneath us. The shelves shook. Manuscripts and voodoo dolls tumbled to the floor.

We backed away from the monster, back and back and

back—until there was no farther back to go.

Behind us stood a huge bay window. In front of us? An abominable snowman, charging like a freight train.

"Get down!" I screamed, tugging Champ out of the way as the monster hurtled toward us—and then straight *past* us, blasting through the window in an explosion of broken glass.

The gigantic snowman landed on the lawn with a deafening thump and stormed into the night. I stared at the hole in the wall where the window used to be.

Hannah glared at both of us, like somehow this was *our* fault! "My dad's gonna kill me," she said, sounding more irritated than anything else. Then she snatched the manuscript away from me and ran outside—I guess, to chase after the monster.

"Too bad about her dad, but, uh, Zach?" Champ was wheezing and sputtering, having a tough time forming words. But he finally found the ones he was looking for. "What. The. Heck. Was. *That?*"

I thought it was pretty clear. It was a fifteen-foot-tall abominable snowman that had somehow jumped out of a book and into our town. He was probably off looking for some people to eat. And for some reason, instead of shrieking and screaming and running away like a normal person, Hannah was running *toward* him.

What could I do but follow her?

CHAPTER 13

I figured we could track Hannah by tracking the monster, and that didn't turn out to be too hard. He had cut a path of destruction through the neighborhood—blaring car alarms, smashed fences, crumpled garbage cans. There were dogs going nuts, their owners looking totally panicked—and there was Hannah, rounding the block and leaping gracefully over a downed tree.

"Hannah! Wait!"

"Go home, Zach!" she called over her shoulder without even slowing down. "You're in over your head."

I sped up and managed to catch her, jogging by her side. "You want to tell me what's going on?"

"Can't explain. Gotta go."

Then *she* sped up, which would have been no problem. Except suddenly Champ flung himself at me and wrapped his arms around my waist.

"Dude, get *off*!"

By the time I managed to shake him, Hannah was long gone.

"Listen very carefully," Champ said. "That's the *Abominable* Snowman of Pasadena. You don't get that nickname by accident. And it just crawled out of a book. That doesn't happen."

Yeah, no kidding.

"I'm going after Hannah," I told him, and took off again, following the sound of car alarms and dog howls.

"I read what he did to Pasadena!" Champ called after me. "No joke!"

I've got to hand it to the guy—he was clearly scared out of his mind, but he refused to leave me behind. We ran together through the deserted streets of Madison, signs of destruction everywhere we looked. It was like a tornado had ripped its way through the town. A tornado with fangs and a really bad attitude.

We tracked the monster all the way to the Madison ice rink. *Of course!* Where else would a snowman go but the coldest place in town? He had torn an entire section of fence off its hinges and shattered the nearest window. Hannah was already there, climbing through.

Champ grabbed me before I could join her. "I've been thinking about it, and—setting the monster aside—I really think we should give Hannah her space."

I shook him off again—I was getting pretty good at that—and hoisted myself up to the window.

"My dad always says, 'Women need their space!'" he shouted after me.

I squeezed through, trying to avoid the jagged glass.

The ice rink was deserted—or at least it seemed that way. But the monster had clearly been here. Smashed arcade games lay on their sides, crushed benches littered the ice, broken glass crunched beneath every footstep. Claw marks had shredded the walls. But there was no snowman—and no Hannah.

"We should call the cops," Champ said in a low voice as we crept toward the ice.

"Have you *met* the cops in this town?"

Champ sighed. "Fair enough."

I hesitated for a moment, and he walked right into me. "A little space?"

"Totally get it," he said. "My bad."

But when we started walking again, I could feel him back there like my shadow, just millimeters behind me.

"This is one of the top five stupidest things I've ever done," he complained.

We both jumped at the sound of an explosion. I dropped to my knees and gazed frantically around. It took me a few seconds to see it was a burst soda can, fizzing with Coke.

I climbed up quickly and spotted Hannah standing dead center on the ice. She was spinning slowly in place, holding the open book in front of her like some kind of shield.

Or some kind of weapon.

Champ snorted. "What's she gonna do? Read it a story?"

We slip-slid our way toward her, feet skidding out from under us every few steps. My breath was coming out in steamy puffs, and my toes were instantly numb. This place was *cold*: definitely abominable snowman territory. So where was he?

Once again, Hannah didn't look very pleased to see us. I was starting to think she wasn't exactly the getting-rescued type.

"What's happening?" I asked her. "How did that thing just pop out of a book?"

"Shhh!" she hissed. "It's in here."

No kidding, I thought.

"We should get a gun," Champ suggested.

"A gun? We need a *tank*!" I said.

"Wait. He's made out of snow!" Champ said excitedly.

"Flamethrower?"

"Bag of salt!"

"Shhh!" Hannah said again. "It can't be killed."

That wasn't the best news. In the unhappy silence that followed, something dropped on the ice with a tiny ping. I knelt, trying not to fall, and picked it up.

"An M&M?"

Another one dropped. Then another. Suddenly it was raining M&M's.

And Snickers.

And Reese's Peanut Butter Cups.

Champ snatched a 3 Musketeers. "Uh . . . guys?"

We all looked up—just in time to see a vending machine hurtling through the air straight down on us!

CHAPTER 14

"*Looook* out!"

We dove in three directions, skidding across the rink as the huge machine slammed into the ice.

The gigantic snowman followed, landing with a *crash* on the vending machine. Then he scrabbled through the heap of candy like he was digging for treasure.

I felt almost hypnotized by the thing. He was so big . . . so powerful . . . so *snowy*.

"Come on," I said, shaking myself out of it. "It's distracted."

Hannah didn't move.

So I took one arm, Champ took the other, and we yanked.

"You don't understand!" she protested as we dragged her to safety. "The only way to stop him is to suck him back into the book."

"New plan," Champ suggested, still moving away from the creature as quickly as he could. "Leave the book open, we'll run away, it'll suck itself back in. Job well done."

"No!" Hannah pulled herself out of our grasp. "I'm not close enough!" She unlocked the manuscript with a loud click.

Too loud. The snowman turned in our direction, growling at the sight of the book.

Then he came for us.

Hannah didn't back away. She held the book out in front of her, returning the snowman's fierce glare.

"What is she *doing*?" Champ cried.

"Just wait," Hannah said, in a steady voice.

"Hannah, open the book!" I urged. The monster was thudding closer and closer.

"Not yet," Hannah murmured. "Almost there . . . almost . . . *now!*"

She opened the book. The wind kicked up again, this time a funnel sucking everything in toward the pages.

Yes. Yes. It was working. It was pulling the creature closer . . . closer . . .

But then the monster raised his giant, hairy arm the size of a construction girder—and smacked the book out of her hands. It went flying across the rink.

Hannah lunged for the book, and the monster lunged for Hannah. He slammed his massive fist into the ice. The rink shuddered so hard she lost her footing and stumbled.

Now there was nothing to stop the snowman from getting his hands on the book—nothing but me.

I spotted a pile of hockey sticks and grabbed the closest

one. Then I skidded toward the book. *SMACK!* I knocked it as far across the rink as I could. The snowman leaped for it, but snagged himself on a goal net.

While the monster disentangled himself, I pulled Hannah off the ice, and we ran for the book together.

"Guys!" Champ shouted.

We turned around: Champ was sitting at the wheel of a Zamboni machine. The engine roared.

"Good idea!" I shouted.

And then the Zamboni started moving across the ice . . . about as fast as a turtle.

"Bad idea!" I corrected myself, as the abominable snowman shrugged off the goal net and stomped his way toward the Zamboni. "Get off that thing!"

Champ abandoned ship just as the snowman smashed it with one big, hairy punch.

Champ tumbled off the ice and into the penalty box on the sidelines. The snowman roared and turned his attention toward Hannah and me.

"Run!" I cried.

This time, she listened. We skidded across the ice, trying not to look back—but you didn't have to look back to know the monster was close. I could feel his hot, putrid breath on my back.

"In here!" Champ shouted, waving wildly from the penalty box.

The snowman was closing in. There was no way we could outrun him. But maybe . . .

I yanked on Hannah's arm, hard, and we both dropped to the ice. Momentum carried us forward in a baseball slide, and we slammed straight into the penalty box, safe behind its thick Plexiglas door.

Seconds later, the snowman crashed toward us, slamming his head into the door. He unleashed a deafening roar of pain—then passed out cold.

Not so abominable now, are you? I thought.

We were safe . . . for about five seconds. Then the snowman woke up.

"AAAAAAAAH!" he roared.

"AAAAAAAAAH!" we screamed.

The monster pounded his fists against the Plexiglas, which couldn't stand up to his impossible might. Tiny cracks spider-webbed their way across the door. It was only a matter of time, and we had nowhere left to run.

"Stop!" a voice boomed.

It was Shivers.

Shivers, standing in the center of the ice, holding the book wide open. A tornado of wind erupted from the pages with a giant sucking sound, pulling the snarling snowman toward it.

The monster dug his claws into the ice, desperately trying to battle the vacuum, but it was no use.

I gaped in disbelief. The closer the creature got to

the book, the fuzzier he got, almost like he was melting into . . . *ink*? Fur and fangs faded out, resolving into letters, which swirled back onto the page.

And then, just like that, he was gone.

Shivers slammed the book shut.

Every muscle in my body unclenched. I let out a loud, long sigh. I'd never been so relieved.

That is, I was relieved until I saw the look Shivers was shooting at us. Then I kind of wished I could trade him for the abominable snowman.

"All of you," Shivers growled in a murderous voice. "In the car. *Now.*"

CHAPTER 15

I felt like a six-year-old, slumped in the backseat of Shivers's Wagoneer, waiting to get yelled at.

Champ was fidgeting beside me, while Hannah sat up in the front, staring at the window, probably trying to pretend she was anywhere else. I know I was.

He kept us waiting a long time. The guy knew how to build suspense.

"What are you gonna do to us?" Champ finally got up the nerve to ask.

Shivers didn't turn his eyes from the road. *"Silence."*

Champ leaned toward my ear. "We can't ask questions?" he whispered loudly. "Seems like—"

Shivers exploded.

Hannah spoke for the first time since we'd left the rink. "Dad, they were only trying to help."

He slammed a fist down on the steering wheel, and I wondered whether maybe this was a conversation we should postpone until the car stopped moving. Or until, like, never.

Shivers's eyes flickered toward mine in the rearview mirror. "I told you that if you didn't stay away from us, something bad would happen. That's the problem with kids today—they don't listen." He shook his head. "You had to pick *The Abominable Snowman of Pasadena*? Couldn't have picked *Little Shop of Hamsters*?"

The pieces were all falling into place, and it was suddenly pretty obvious what was going on here. Well, maybe not the part about monsters jumping out of books and into Madison, Delaware, but the rest of it.

"You're him, aren't you?" I said. "You're R.L. Stine."

He didn't flinch. "I don't even know who that is."

But I wasn't about to let him get away with that, not after what he and his stupid monster had put us through. "Well, just as well," I said. "Because his books *stink*."

"Whose books?" Champ asked, confused.

Hannah glanced at me, finger sliding across her throat in a cut-it-out motion, but I was too close to quit. I was doing exactly what she'd tried to do earlier—catching the monster with his own books.

"I can't decide which one I hate more," I mused, biting back a smile, "*Monster Blood* or *Go Eat Worms!*?"

Hannah slouched in her seat, giving up on me.

"I'm so confused," Champ said.

But Shivers—I mean, *Stine*—knew exactly what I was talking about. "I mean, you see the endings coming from a mile away," I said. And then, the fatal blow. "It's like, stop trying to be Stephen King, man."

Bingo. Stine slammed on the brakes. The car skidded to a stop. He whipped around in the seat, fixing me with one of those killer glares of his, but he couldn't scare me anymore.

Well, not much, anyway.

"Who are you to talk about Stephen King?" he snapped. "I—"

Hannah grabbed his arm. "Dad, please calm down."

He muttered some words I couldn't hear under his breath. Then he shrugged and took his foot off the brake. The car started moving again, this time way too fast.

"Dad?" Hannah said nervously. "Your face is doing that red thing again."

That just made him bear down harder on the gas. His fingers squeezed the wheel so hard they turned white.

And Champ finally caught up with the rest of us. "No *way*," he said, bouncing in his seat. "You're R.L. Stine? That's you? You're famous! Really? *Really?*"

Champ was having some kind of fit, bouncing so hard that his head nearly hit the ceiling. "R.L. Stine! Oh, man! I never do this, but can I get a picture for my Instagram?" Without waiting for an answer, he pulled out his phone and shoved it in front of Stine's face, grinning for a selfie.

The flash was blinding—and not just for me. Stine nearly swerved off the road. "What the heck are you doing!" he roared, steering back into the right lane.

"Sorry." Champ didn't sound sorry. And he certainly didn't *look* sorry. "Just wanted to get a photo."

"Oh, can I see it?" Stine asked, suddenly polite.

Champ handed over the phone—and Stine tossed it out the window.

That was the end of conversation.

It was an endless, silent ride back to my house. Finally, Stine pulled into my driveway, and we all climbed out.

"So what happens now?" I asked him.

His eyebrows knit together in a vicious V. "You go home, put on your pj's, get your blankie, go nap-nap, and in the morning, tonight will just feel like a bad dream."

For a kids book author, he *really* seemed to have a problem with kids.

He hustled Hannah into the house before we could even say good-bye . . . so we went in right after them. Stine was so angry, he didn't even notice.

"Go upstairs and pack your bags!" he shouted at her. "We need to get out of here before people start asking questions." He strode across the room to the flat-screen TV and swung it out from the wall. There was a giant hole in the plaster, and Stine reached inside to grab a suitcase.

Hannah paused on the stairs, spotting me and Champ in the doorway. Then she took a deep breath. "I don't wanna go," she told her father.

I got the feeling it was the first time she'd ever dared talk

back to him.

"I like it here," she said quietly.

His voice softened. "Honey, you have to understand—"

"I don't have to understand anything!" she shouted. "I just want to be normal for once!"

Stine totally ignored her. He was staring at the floor, counting footsteps like he was following a treasure map or something. And maybe he was, because then he stamped hard on a floorboard and it popped open. Beneath it was a pile of credit cards, passports, and a whole lot of cash.

"We're not a normal family," he told Hannah, rifling through the cards. "Now pack your things."

I stood there in the doorway, silently rooting for her to fight back some more. But instead, she headed over to the fireplace and reached her hand up into the flue. She pulled out a duffel bag.

Had these people never heard of closets?

"I am so over this," Hannah snapped.

Stine growled something under his breath. It sounded like, "Teenagers."

Maybe if Hannah couldn't convince him, I should give it a try.

I took a couple steps into the house.

A couple noisy steps, I guess, because Stine snapped up at the sound, grabbed a candelabra—and hurled it straight at my head.

CHAPTER 16

Or, rather, about ten feet to the left of my head.

"I could've killed you!" Stine said when he realized it was me.

I laughed, looking at the dent in the wall halfway across the room. "Luckily, your aim is terrible."

"Why are you still here?" he asked, in a tone that suggested he didn't care about the answer. "Go home!"

"No." Even if she came with a terrifying monster and an even more terrifying dad, I wasn't ready to say good-bye to Hannah forever. Also, I really did want some answers. "Not until you explain what's going on."

"I can't explain it."

"We were almost just eaten by Frosty the Snowman!" I yelled. "So . . . try."

It was a miracle, but he actually did. "Okay, look, when I was younger, I suffered from terrible allergies that forced me indoors," he said, pushing his glasses up higher on his nose.

I squinted, trying to imagine a younger, nerdier version of Stine. But that was the thing about grown-ups—it was

impossible to see them as anything but old.

"The other kids would throw rocks at my window and call me names," he continued. "So I made up my own friends—monsters, demons, ghouls—that would terrorize my town and all the kids that ever made fun of me."

Now, *that* sounded more like the Stine I'd come to know and loathe.

"They became real to me," he said. "And then, one day, they actually . . . *became real*. My monsters literally leaped off the page! As long as the books stay locked, we're safe. But when they open . . . well, you just saw what happened."

It was totally, utterly unbelievable. But given what I'd just seen, I had to believe it.

"I'm allergic to dust mites," Champ said suddenly.

"What?"

"I'm just saying, I have allergies, too, so I understand."

Telling his story seemed to have used up all the strength Stine had left. He didn't even bother to tell Champ to shut up. "I've already told you too much," he said, sounding defeated. "Hannah, come on."

He marched up the stairs without even waiting to see if she would obey him.

She did, of course. When she headed up the stairs, Champ and I followed her. All the way to the room at the end of the dark hallway, Stine's study, where it all began.

"Hannah, grab A to M," Stine ordered, starting to pull

books off the shelves. "I'll grab N to Z. And keep the man-eating plant away from the bug-eyed aliens. You know how—" He stopped, freezing with his hand on one of the spines. "Wait. The manuscripts. One of them is missing!"

It wasn't exactly the mystery of the century. I pointed to where *Night of the Living Dummy* was lying on the floor.

It was only when Stine picked it up, his face melting into a look of pure horror, that I realized the lock was broken. "No," he whispered. "Not him . . ."

I knew the book was about a ventriloquist's dummy. It was hard to get too worked up about a silly wooden doll after we'd conquered the abominable snowman.

That's when the laughter started. High, almost childlike laughter, echoing through the house.

The black leather chair at Stine's desk slowly spun around to face us.

"No!" Stine screamed. "No! Please—no!"

CHAPTER 17

"Hello, Papa."

It was just a dummy, sure . . . except there was nothing *just* about it.

The thing was less than three feet high, but from its fathomless black eyes to the wicked grin carved across its cheeks, it oozed pure evil. It had thick black eyebrows and a swoop of black hair, just like Stine.

"How long has it been?" the dummy said, its jaw clacking together with every word.

"Not long enough," Stine muttered.

"Feels like *forever* to me," the dummy rasped. Its eyes slid back and forth. "Who are your new friends?"

Champ and I each took one big step away from Stine.

"We're not friends," I said quickly.

"Barely know him."

Stine smiled stiffly at the dummy. "Slappy, it's so, er, nice to see you."

"Didja miss me?" the dummy asked.

"Of course I've missed you! As much as I missed that

cold sore I had last week."

Lightning flashed, blinding us all for a second. When my eyes adjusted to the dark again, Slappy was perched on the edge of Stine's desk. The key to the manuscripts dangled from his hand.

"Now I can see you better," the dummy said. "So, what's the plan, friend? You must've brought me out for something fun. Terrorize the locals? Destroy the town? Let's get silly."

Stine picked up *Night of the Living Dummy* and crept toward Slappy *verrrrry* slowly. "Yes, Slappy," he said, holding the manuscript behind his back. "You've guessed it. I want to destroy Madison. And I couldn't do it without you."

"Aw, shucks, you're giving me—what's the word? Goosebumps!"

The dummy giggled. It was like nails on a chalkboard.

"Oh my god, he's so creepy," Champ whispered. It was the understatement of the century.

"You always crack me up," Stine said, closing in on Slappy. "I'd like to crack you up, too. Into wood chips."

"You're so funny," Slappy replied. "Remind me to laugh later. Is that really your face? Or did you throw up on your neck?"

I held my breath. Just a few more steps . . .

"Such a clever dummy," Stine murmured.

The bushy wooden eyebrows pivoted into an angry

expression. "Who you calling dummy, *dummy*?" Slappy's eyes locked onto the manuscript. His voice flew to an even higher pitch. "You trying to put me back in?"

Stine laughed an extremely unconvincing laugh. "Don't be silly, Slappy. Not when our visit is just starting. Stay right there." He opened the book.

"Know how I can tell when you're lying to me, Papa?" Slappy said. "It's whenever you speak. You lie more than a shag rug."

Suddenly, the overhead light snuffed out, dropping us into darkness.

A moment later, Slappy lit a match.

Let's just say flickering fire didn't make the guy look *less* creepy.

Slappy sat on the edge of the broken window, the *Night of the Living Dummy* manuscript somehow in his hand. "I'm not going back on the shelf," he rasped. *"Ever. Again."*

He waved the manuscript in the air. "I love a good story," he said. "A good book like this lights a flame in my heart."

"Wait, Slappy, don't!" Stine cried as Slappy touched the match to the manuscript. It began to burn.

Slappy dropped the flaming pages out the window. "I think it's *my turn* to pull the strings!" he cackled. "Tonight is gonna be the best story you ever wrote. *All* your children are coming out to play. Too bad you won't be alive to read it!"

CHAPTER 18

Another flash of lightning made me cry out. A crash of thunder. I blinked in the sudden darkness.

When the lights came back on, Slappy was gone.

"OMG," Champ breathed. "He left."

"OMG, he left," Stine said. But he didn't sound quite as relieved.

Then we all realized what he was staring at, and understood why.

"He took all the books!" Hannah shouted.

We ran downstairs, thinking maybe we could catch Slappy. He was a three-foot-tall dummy, after all. How fast could he go?

Fast enough, apparently.

Stine stopped at the door and buried his head in his hands. "Congratulations. You just released a cruel, destructive, vicious, brilliant ventriloquist dummy with a serious Napoleon complex."

It took a second to realize he was talking to *me*.

And one more second to get indignant.

"For the record, I only opened *one* book," I reminded him. "I wouldn't even have done that if someone had just explained the situation to me rather than yelling a bunch of vague threats about bad things and doom!"

"The snowman knocked a few books to the ground when he got out," Hannah said. "The lock must have broken."

I mouthed a silent *thank-you* to her for trying, not that it helped much.

"I'm still blaming him," Stine said, jabbing a finger at me. "I don't like you, boy."

Never in the history of time had a feeling been more mutual.

Stine tried to storm out, but the door stuck, which kind of ruined the effect. "It's locked from the outside."

That was . . . not good.

I tried a window—no luck. "Locked."

Something shimmied past us in the dark. A hulking shadow appeared on the wall behind us.

I decided I was never opening another book as long as I lived.

"Out the kitchen door," Stine urged us. "Go. Now!"

We stopped dead in the kitchen entryway. The back door had a small doggy flap at the bottom, and it swung open. Standing before it stood a little man in an elf costume. *Huh?* Wait. I realized I was staring at a lawn gnome!

I almost laughed. All that panic . . . for a lawn gnome?

Even Champ wasn't intimidated. He stepped in front of us. "This one's mine." But before he could toss the gnome out of the house, the dishwasher door popped open, issuing a billow of steam—and two more gnomes.

Champ stepped back into line. "I, uh, thought there was just one."

The ugly little creatures began appearing everywhere.

One popped out of the trash can. Another peeked out of the cupboard door. Five more leaped out of the drawers, and I was pretty sure I spotted some beady eyes blinking at me from beneath the sink. Before we knew it, we were surrounded.

Still, I thought, *what's the big deal?* Sure, we were surrounded, but we were surrounded by porcelain *gnomes*.

"What's everyone so scared about?" I asked. "They're just cute little garden—*aaah!*" A knife zinged straight past my ear, stabbing the wall behind me.

The gnome closest to me pulled out another shining blade. His eyes glowed red, and I caught the cruel, cold scowl on his bearded face.

"Oh," I said.

One of the gnomes launched itself at Stine, wrapping its little arms around its head and swatting his ears. A second one attached itself to his waist.

"Ahhh!" Stine whacked at them, to no effect. "Get them

off me!"

I grabbed a frying pan and slammed it at the gnome on Stine's face—just as Champ smashed a rolling pin into the other one.

Good news. The gnomes fell off.

Bad news, Stine fell over, howling in pain.

Oops.

Before Stine could climb to his feet, a group of gnomes dragged in a garden hose and started tying up his legs. A battalion grabbed his ankles and started dragging him toward the kitchen oven. Tiny hands spun the heat up to 500 degrees. Stine squirmed and screamed.

Champ and I struggled to fight our way toward him.

Hannah shoved a gnome off her father and rammed it into the garbage disposal, face first. Porcelain shards showered the kitchen.

"Ouch!" I shouted. "That hurts." I grabbed a Swiffer.

"Uh, Zach, we can clean up later," Champ said. But I was already swinging it like a golf club, cracking every porcelain head I could find.

Champ crawled through my legs and tried to untie Stine. I whacked another gnome, then looked for more—but there weren't any. We'd smashed them all!

"Victory over lawn gnomes!" Champ crowed. "And . . ." He gestured at his suit, which was covered in a fine dusting of porcelain powder. ". . . I did it in style. Designer suit.

Fifty percent off."

I took a few deep breaths, trying to wrap my head around the fact that we were still all in one piece.

Stine hugged Hannah. Hannah hugged me. I hugged Champ, and when Champ hugged Stine, the author didn't even complain.

I guess we were all a little giddy with our triumph. Until there was a scratching sound beneath us—the sound of porcelain pieces rattling back to life.

Slowly at first, then faster and faster, the pieces skidded toward one another like magnets, re-forming into gnomes. They were chipped and dented—and they were angry.

"Nooooo," Champ moaned. "No, no, nononono!"

CHAPTER 19

"We have to get out of here!" I said, though that was pretty obvious. "We need to get to the basement."

"It's locked," Stine said.

Uh . . .

"I broke the lock," I admitted.

"That's vandalism, young man."

I was already racing for the cellar door. "Send me a bill!" I shouted over my shoulder.

The gnomes chased us across the house as we headed for the basement, nearly trampling one another on our way down the stairs.

"Watch out for the bear traps!" Stine cried, just in time.

We hopscotched across the traps. The herd of gnomes stampeded down the stairs. It seemed like there were more of them than ever. But unlike us, they didn't know about the traps. One gnome after another stepped in between those iron jaws and exploded into a cloud of porcelain shards.

It wouldn't stop them—we knew that now. But it would slow them down enough for us to escape.

Hopefully.

We raced up the stairs to the outside and burst through the cellar door. Gasping for air, Stine slammed the door behind us and fastened the padlock.

I would have said something about how he should try to stay in better shape . . . but I was panting too hard to talk.

We all stood there on the lawn for a moment, sucking air into our lungs and wondering what we should do next.

"Why couldn't you have written stories about rainbows and unicorns?" I asked Stine, once I recovered the power of speech.

"Because that doesn't sell four hundred million copies!"

"Domestic?" Champ asked.

Stine looked away. "No, worldwide. Still very impressive. Shut up."

There was only a sliver of moon, and the snowman had knocked out all the streetlights, but I could see everyone's faces pretty clearly. Because the air around us was swarming with millions of tiny lights, like fireflies.

On any other night, it might have been beautiful. On that night? It could only mean that something else was going wrong.

We followed the glowing cloud to its source—a smoldering pile of what had once been leather-bound manuscripts.

Stine's jaw dropped open.

"He's burning the books," Hannah said.

I didn't get it. "Why is he doing that?"

"So there's no way to put the monsters back inside," Stine said, sounding like it was the end of the world.

Given all those books—and all those monsters—maybe it *was* the end of the world.

"This is Slappy's revenge," Stine said. Then, just for a moment, he brightened. "*Slappy's Revenge*—hey, that's a good title."

The man bent over his bike, pedaling hard into the wind. He didn't even hear the car approaching behind him . . . not until it pulled close enough for him to smell its exhaust. Its headlights lit the road stretching ahead of him. Its engine roared. "Go around!" the man shouted, waving his arm. "Cyclists' rights!"

The car didn't speed up or swerve around him. It kept shadowing him, its lights blazing brighter against the night.

The cyclist glanced over his shoulder, nearly blinded by flashing high beams.

The man raised a fist. "I'm a lawyer and I will sue!"

The car swerved abruptly, running him off the road, straight into a ditch. The cyclist lay silent and motionless.

Inside the car, wooden hands gripped the steering wheel. Wooden teeth clattered together.

Slappy laughed. "I'm sorry; I cut you off. Someday I should take a driving lesson! But why bother? My feet don't reach the pedals! Ha-ha-ha!"

Slappy drove on. He liked this town. He had big plans for it.

The car window rolled down, and a burning manuscript flew through it, flames showering blazing tracks through the night.

The road was deserted—there was no one to see the green tendrils sprouting from its pages, each one lined with razor-sharp, man-eating teeth.

The tendrils grew with breathtaking speed. Soon they were climbing their way up cell towers, snaking their way through and around the town, slowly but surely cutting off Madison from the outside world and whatever help it could provide.

Slappy drove on. Manuscripts burned and fireballs danced across the highway, each of them unleashing a great and terrible beast on the unsuspecting town.

In the distance, a woman screamed. Slappy giggled. There would be plenty to laugh about once this night was over. And plenty of delicious screams.

Slappy was just getting started.

CHAPTER 20

We drove all over town, searching for Slappy.

We didn't find him. All we found was destruction. Smoking ruins, people screaming . . . the town looked like a war zone.

I kept trying to call my mom, Aunt Lorraine, anyone. But it was no use.

"I can't get reception," I reported, after the tenth try returned yet another busy signal.

"Slappy's taking out all the cell towers," Stine said. "That's what I'd do if I were him."

Stine didn't seem all that bothered that he was in sync with a criminally insane dummy.

"He's cutting us off," Stine went on. "Isolating us."

There was a loud thud on the hood of the car.

"What was that?" Champ asked in a trembling voice.

We all peered through the windshield into darkness: Nothing.

A second later, two handprints appeared on the windshield.

Stine gulped. "It's the Invisible Boy! He's a menace!"

Whatever was out there scampered onto the roof. We could hear him dancing around up there.

Then Champ jerked back, as if something had reached through the open window and slapped him hard. *"Ow!"* he yelped.

Suddenly, he was yanked off the seat by his tie. His head ricocheted back with one invisible slap after another. He swatted the air uselessly. It would have been hilarious if it hadn't been so terrifying. "Help!" he screamed, whacking at empty space. "Help me! Help!"

Stine slammed on the brakes, and whatever was clinging to the car landed hard on the grass, grunting at the impact.

"I think we're safe now," Stine said, then pushed the pedal to the floor. Better not to take any chances.

Above us, there was a thud.

Then another.

"Probably just some debris we can't see," Stine suggested.

"For sure," Hannah agreed.

"Definitely not the invisible kid," Champ said.

Before we could worry about the noises on the roof that were definitely, hopefully, possibly not the Invisible Boy coming to rip our heads off, we turned into the town square—and stopped.

Hannah gasped. "What the—"

"Hannah, language," Stine said automatically, but you knew he was thinking the same thing. We all were.

Main Street was a frozen ruin. Downed telephone lines sizzled on the concrete. Shattered streetlights bent at crazy angles over silent streets. Fire hydrants spewed water. Something had taken a giant bite out of the statue of the town founder.

The square wasn't empty . . . not quite. There were about a dozen people scattered around—but none of them were moving, not even a little. Not even to breathe.

Something had turned them into statues.

Champ leaped out of the car and raced toward one of the frozen figures. "Oh my god, Dad! Dad! What have they— oh." He laughed, then patted the frozen man on the shoulder. "Oops. That's not my dad."

I wondered whether the people were alive or dead, whether they were watching us through terrified, frozen eyes, waiting for us to do something—to save them.

"What are we going to do?" Hannah said, reaching out to one of the women, stopping just before her finger came to rest on the woman's frozen tear.

I'd never felt so helpless.

Stine must have felt even worse. He was the one who'd written all these monsters into existence. Whatever they did, he must have felt like it was his fault. He sighed. "Without those manuscripts, there's nothing I can do."

Suddenly, I had an idea. "If you wrote the monsters *off* the page, then maybe there's a way you could write them

back *on* the page."

He shook his head. "Do you know how many stories I'd have to write to capture every monster I ever created? I already have carpal tunnel in both hands—and my neck!"

He didn't get it. "Just *one*," I explained. "One story to capture them all!"

"Oh, just one?" he said, sarcasm dripping from his voice. "One story with every creature I've ever created? Great plan!"

"You have a better idea?"

I waited for him to propose one.

But Stine was obviously out of ideas—everyone was. It was try mine, or give up, go home, and wait to get eaten by a carnivorous frog or whatever else Stine and Slappy had in store for us.

So I made the decision for him. For all of us.

"We need to get you to a computer so you can start writing. Here, we'll break into that computer store."

Champ looked excited at the idea of getting his hands on some shiny new tech, but Stine shook his head again. "No, I need my typewriter. All my stories were written on that Smith Corona! It's not just me. That typewriter . . . It's special. It has a soul of its own. If I write on anything else, it won't matter."

At least he was on board. Was it possible we actually had the beginnings of a real plan?

"Where's the typewriter?" I asked.

"Don't worry," Stine assured us. "It's in a safe place."

Just one problem: That night, there were no safe places left.

CHAPTER 21

Turned out the typewriter was in a display case down at the high school. Apparently, we were going to the dance after all. Which was fine with me—if there were monsters tearing the town apart, I needed to make sure my mom was okay.

We sped toward the school, none of us much in the mood to chat. It's tough to make small talk when you're pretty sure a horde of monsters is tearing apart your town and you're the only people with any hope of stopping them, even if it means you'll probably die trying.

I was trying not to dwell too much on that last part, though, so I figured I'd try to lighten the mood.

"So, Hannah," I said, all casual. She twisted around in her seat, probably expecting me to have something earth-shattering, or at least monster-related, to say. "Not sure how the rest of your night looks, but we might hit up this dance."

It was small, but it was a smile. "*Hmm* . . . I'll have to check my schedule."

Suddenly, there was a hand between us—a thick, calloused hand that looked extremely Stine-like. He waved it in between us until Hannah turned around to face front.

Stine took his eyes off the road just long enough to glare at me. "Stop talking to my daughter, or I'll lock you in the trunk. Don't think I won't—"

"Look out!" Champ pointed at two people standing in the middle of the street—right in front of our car. Stine swerved hard to the left, but it was too late. We rammed straight into them . . . and straight through them, into a telephone pole.

We screamed as metal crunched and squealed. The car's hood crumpled around the pole.

The people we'd swerved to avoid were glowing and transparent in the moonlight. *Ghosts*.

"Is everyone okay?" Stine asked. Gingerly, I tested my arms and legs. Shaking and shuddery, but all in one piece.

Too bad we couldn't say the same for the car.

"What's a telephone pole doing in the middle of the street?" I complained.

"Uh . . ." Champ pointed up through the sunroof. "I don't think that's a telephone pole."

We looked up—and up, and up. The pole stretched at least thirty feet high.

Champ was right: It wasn't a pole at all.

It was a leg . . . attached to a giant insect torso . . . attached to a fifty-foot-tall praying mantis!

CHAPTER 22

A praying mantis that was bowing its head in our direction, jaws gaping wide.

"I don't remember writing about a giant praying mantis," Stine mused as the rest of us screamed our heads off.

The mantis spit out a splatter of green mucus the size of an elephant. Mantis gunk plastered the windshield, encasing us in the dark.

Outside, we could hear a primal hiss, low and crackly, like an egg sizzling on the world's biggest frying pan.

"Right." Stine nodded sharply. "Now I remember."

"Get us *out* of here," I suggested. "Now!"

He turned on the windshield wipers. *Seriously?*

"What are you doing?" I screeched.

"Well, I can't drive if I can't see!"

While the wiper smeared green slime back and forth across the windshield, Stine threw the car into reverse, and then into drive. We sped away from the mantis. We could hear it pounding concrete behind us, the road cracking beneath its massive weight. Stine swerved back and forth between its gigantic legs.

"They've all turned against me!" he complained. "It's like Frankenstein's monster turning on Frankenstein!"

"It's above us!" Hannah cried as the mantis hissed again.

Thick splats of mantis mucus rained down on the sunroof.

"And behind us!" I shouted as another leg stomped down inches from the car's trunk.

"It's everywhere!" Champ whispered in despair.

"Everyone shut up, or I will pull this car over right now!" Stine warned.

Instead of pulling over, he sped up, bouncing over a curb and into a supermarket parking lot, faster and faster until we barreled hard into a parked car. Only my seat belt kept me from flying through the windshield.

Air bags exploded into our faces, and the car filled with smoke. We piled out, fast as we could, as the mantis closed in.

"In here!" Hannah cried.

We threw ourselves through the supermarket door just as the mantis snatched the car by its hood and tore off the roof. It screeched in frustration when it discovered we weren't inside, then tossed the car across the parking lot.

I closed my eyes and ducked beneath the checkout counter, thinking: *Could have been us.*

"Why'd you have to come up with something so bizarre?" Champ whined. "Why, Stine? Why?!"

"Just have a knack for it, I guess." He sounded almost

proud.

The mantis leaped toward the overturned car and stomped on it, crushing it to a pancake.

"My Wagoneer!" Stine cried. He seemed more dismayed by this than anything that had happened all night. "It had such low mileage!"

Fortunately, the praying mantis had a taste for cars, and the parking lot was full of them. It hopped from car to car, having fun shaking them in the air and then crushing them flat.

It might have been playing—or it might just have been looking for us.

CHAPTER
23

The supermarket lights were on and its Muzak was playing full blast, but the place was deserted. Everyone sane was probably at home, hiding under their beds.

"How far are we from the high school?" I asked.

"Not too far," Hannah said. "We can cut through the cemetery."

A *cemetery*? "You've gotta be kidding me."

She shrugged. "The high school is just past the woods on the other side."

Stine narrowed his eyes. "How do you know that?"

"Well . . ." Hannah looked like she'd said something she hadn't meant to. "Sometimes I get a little stir-crazy and go exploring."

"When?"

"At night," she admitted. "After you go to bed."

It didn't seem like such a big deal, especially after everything that had happened, but to Stine, it was a big deal.

"You're grounded!" he shouted.

"That is so unfair!" Hannah shouted back.

I rolled my eyes. "Um, you guys are both bringing up good points, but let's keep moving while you argue."

As long we were in the market, I figured we might as well grab some supplies. Stine snagged a bag of chips. Champ gazed at a towering display of soda bottles.

"Hey, you got a dollar I could borrow?" he asked Stine.

"What? No. Why?"

"I'm really thirsty! I need a soda."

Stine sighed. "Just take one. It's an emergency. They'll understand."

"Really?" You could see Champ weighing it in his mind. "I kinda want a Coke. Maybe a Gatorade, though . . ."

Stine snatched a Pepsi off the rack and shoved it at Champ. "For god's sake, *here*."

Hannah giggled and wandered toward the granola bars. I followed her.

"I don't know what I was thinking," I said, smiling at her. I mean, sure, we were hiding out in a supermarket while a giant praying mantis waited outside to crush our heads, and we were about to go traipsing through a cemetery, but in the meantime, wasn't I kind of, sort of on a date? "There's way more going on here than New York."

Hannah stopped, turned to me, and—very gently— brushed some hair off my forehead. My skin buzzed at her touch.

"What?" I said, quietly, afraid to do anything to startle

her, ruin the moment. I'd never been this close to a girl before.

"You cut yourself," she said, and then went off in search of a first-aid kit.

"Is it bad?" I asked, once she'd started dabbing at my forehead with a cotton swab. The sting of antiseptic brought tears to my eyes, but I blinked them back. No way did I want her to think I was *crying* over some little cut.

"Yeah, it's really bad."

"Is my face messed up?" I asked, trying not to panic.

"Big-time." She grinned. "It looks exactly the same."

Okay, maybe not the world's most traditional date, but there we were, alone in the supermarket aisle, fluorescents flickering like candlelight, romantic Muzak, her face so close to mine, and in the background, the sound of something growling and gnawing at a bone—

Wait a second.

Hannah looked at me. I looked at her. Then we both turned to look at the meat section . . . where a giant, shaggy werewolf was gnawing on a side of prime rib!

Stine and Champ joined us just as the wolf tossed the rib aside and started gnawing away at a bloody flank steak.

Champ opened his mouth, but I pressed my finger to my lips. Maybe if we were *very* quiet and backed away *very* slowly, we could get out of there before the wolf sniffed out some über-fresh meat.

88

Champ nodded *okay*, then twisted open the cap of his Pepsi.

Hissssssss.

The werewolf swiveled its head toward us. We ran.

Champ and Hannah raced toward the frozen-food section. I headed toward the pet aisle and Stine followed, but he got waylaid in personal hygiene.

"The Werewolf of Fever Swamp can pick up my scent," he explained, smearing himself with Purell. "I need to hide!"

It didn't work. I'd squeezed myself into a cardboard doghouse when I heard Stine whimpering. The wolf was coming straight for him. I didn't stop to think—I just wiggled out of the cardboard house, grabbed a rubber steak from the nearest shelf, and waggled it at the wolf.

"Here, doggy," I called, then threw the steak as far as I could.

Yesss! The werewolf yelped happily and went racing after the rubber steak.

Hannah and Champ dragged Stine to his feet, and then we were off, racing toward the glowing EMERGENCY EXIT lights, trying to ignore the footsteps pounding behind us as the werewolf realized his meat was getting away.

I kicked over a mop bucket, and soapy water went sloshing everywhere. The werewolf slipped and slid, and we ran, throwing ourselves through the back door and into the alleyway.

Stine slammed the steel door shut behind us. "Let's see him get through that!"

CHAPTER 24

About five seconds later, we did. The wolf exploded through the door.

We turned and kept running, down the alley, into the back parking lot—straight into a dead end!

The werewolf unleashed a set of short, halting barks, almost like he was laughing at us. Then he bared his fangs, lowered his head, and prepared to charge.

I couldn't believe it was all going to end here, cornered in a supermarket alley. Chomped to death by a fictional werewolf. "Well, guys, it's been—"

Headlights flooded the alley. A car engine roared. The werewolf turned from us toward the car—just as it steamrolled toward him and battered him straight into a brick wall.

We gaped at the strange car, at the flattened werewolf, and at the driver, who leaned out her window and waved hello.

"I'm okay!" she cried—just as the driver's side airbag popped and knocked her back into the seat.

"Who *is* that?" Hannah asked.

I shook my head. I was confused, shocked, and more than a little impressed. "*That* is my aunt Lorraine."

Aunt Lorraine finally fought her way out of the airbag and climbed out of the car. I'd never seen her without perfect hair and makeup, but now she was a total mess. Her hair was standing straight out from her head, and her dress was coated with what looked like . . . *poodle fur*?

Maybe we weren't the only ones who'd had a strange night.

"Oh my god!" she said, examining the coarse fur crumpled at the side of the car. "I just killed a bear?!"

"It was actually a werewolf," Hannah informed her, sounding as if this sort of thing happened to her every day.

Aunt Lorraine didn't seem surprised.

"Uh, Aunt Lorraine, what are you doing here?" I asked.

"This is the back of my store," she said, pointing to the sign above the alleyway: "Be Dazzled by Lorraine."

"I didn't know where else to go. I can't get hold of your mother or the police or anyone!"

That's when she noticed that Stine was with us. She started patting down her wild hair and gave him a crooked smile, batting her eyelashes. "I don't think we've officially met. My name's Lorraine."

Uh-oh. I knew that smile. I knew those eyelashes. I didn't know whom to be more afraid for—my aunt or Stine.

Neither of them knew what they were getting into.

"R.L. Stine," he said, shaking her hand. "We owe you a debt of gratitude. Your reckless driving saved our lives."

"Thanks!" She tucked a strand of hair behind her ear. "So, Stine, Shivers, whatever . . . you can call me Lorraine or Rainey or—"

"Lorraine!" I cut in. "We don't have time. I need you to drive to the police station and tell them to meet us at the high school. Can you do that?"

She didn't look very happy about it, but she said, "I can do that." Then she whistled in appreciation. "What a night. My horoscope predicted all of this."

Hannah crinkled her forehead. "Your horoscope predicted a monster invasion?"

She shrugged. "Pretty much. It said, 'Prepare yourself for unexpected surprises.'"

None of us could argue with that.

The police headquarters were dark and vacant. A wall of TV monitors revealed the scope of the monstrous destruction: mummies, evil clowns, vampires, a colossal praying mantis with a thing for parked cars.

Inside the station, there was no

movement, no action, no heroes working to save the day. Everything was perfectly still. Abandoned. It felt like the end of the world.

Lorraine crept inside. "Hello? Is anyone here?"

Someone was there. Someone was watching. But he wasn't quite ready for Lorraine to know that. Not yet.

A police radio sat on one of the desks. Lorraine decided to take matters into her own hands. "Calling all cops, calling all cops, head to the high school. My nephew's in trouble. He's with R.L. Stine. They think they know how to stop all this! Can anyone hear me?"

Silence.

And then, there was a voice. But it wasn't coming from the radio.

"I can hear you."

Lorraine turned around slowly.

There in the police chief's chair, wearing the chief's hat, was Slappy.

"Sergeant Slappy," he said, "ready to protect and serve."

Slappy always liked it—the way they looked when they first saw him, the way their faces froze, as if they were made of wood.

"Oh my goodness!" Lorraine squealed. "You're—"

"Don't say it," he warned.

"A talking—"

He gave her one more chance. "Don't do it."

"—dummy."

She was all out of chances. Slappy signaled to the shadows. "You have the right to remain . . ."

A squadron of bug-eyed aliens appeared from the corners of the room, aiming their freeze-ray guns.

"Silent," Slappy said.

The aliens fired.

Lorraine froze in place.

Slappy tossed back his head and cackled. "Bit of a cold spell in here. You look absolutely frozen! Ha-ha!"

As the aliens waited for further command, the station door slid open. A chipped, dented lawn gnome appeared in the entryway. Perfect timing.

"What did Stine do when you attacked him?" Slappy asked eagerly. "Did he cry like a baby and beg for his life?"

Slappy always liked it when they begged.

The gnome said nothing, but Slappy understood, and was enraged. "There were four hundred of you. You couldn't kill a writer?"

This is annoying—but not a disaster, Slappy thought. Then he smiled. Why leave Stine to his slaves? He had a better idea.

"It's like they say: If you want to break an omelet, you have to do it yourself."

CHAPTER 25

The cemetery was the least scary thing I'd seen all night.

Which meant it was still pretty terrifying. The sliver of moon cast shadows in the trees. Stone angels watched our slow progress through the graves.

The only sound was the crunching of leaves beneath our feet and our own steady breathing. I tried not to think about the bodies rotting six feet under.

Stine and Champ led the way, while Hannah and I followed behind, walking side by side, close enough to almost touch. We stayed quiet. It felt comfortable, walking beside her, just being silent.

But soon, Stine and Champ started chatting away. I wondered if they thought their voices could scare away the ghosts.

"So, kid, how'd you get the nickname Champ?" Stine asked.

"It's not a nickname."

He chuckled. "So that's your *real* name? Is it short for something?"

"My full name is . . . Champion."

I swallowed a laugh. Poor Champ.

"My family's a pretty big sports family," Champ explained. "My dad won a bronze at the '92 Olympics and then got a Bronze Star for saving his whole platoon. And my mom was an all-American sprinter and two-time world debate champion. So if you can imagine two athletes like my parents getting married, chances are their kids are gonna be superhumans. So they named me Champ, and I've been disappointing them ever since . . ."

I felt bad for him; I also understood. I knew all about parents who were heroes, parents who made you feel like you had something impossible to live up to.

I was always worried about disappointing my dad, even now that he wasn't around anymore. Maybe it didn't make any sense, but that's how I felt. Like he was waiting for me to do something great.

Stine, big shock, was just a little less understanding. He burst out laughing. "So your full name is *Champion*? That's a name for a horse!" he said. Then he must have seen something on Champ's face, because the laughter stopped cold. "I'm sorry. Bad joke."

Maybe the guy had a soul after all.

"Yeah, well, I'm still young," Champ said. "Plenty of time to be a hero."

Without talking about it, Hannah and I both slowed down a little, lengthening the distance between us and her dad until it almost felt like we were in the graveyard alone. A cloud drifted in front of the moon, blocking its dim light.

"If you're scared, I'll hold your hand," I told her, sort of joking and sort of not.

"Please. You're the scaredy-cat."

"Then maybe you should hold *my* hand."

Her smile turned into a silent scream. Her eyes bulged. She froze in horror as a gray hand grabbed her shoulder. She let out a little shriek, followed by an embarrassed giggle. We both realized she'd just walked into the outstretched hand of a stone angel.

"Give me a sec," I said, trying to untangle her from the stone fingers. "It's caught on your jacket."

I stretched my arms around her, trying to work her coat out of its snag.

"My hero," she whispered.

Her face was only a couple inches from mine. Her lips looked so soft.

"There," I said. Our eyes met. "You're good to go."

She didn't move. Our eyes were locked on each other. *This is it*, I thought, psyching myself up. *This is my moment.* All I had to do was step in, just a little, then a little more, until our lips touched—

I stepped forward—and stumbled over a branch, falling to the ground with a thump.

That's when I realized it wasn't a branch.

It was a muddy hand, reaching out of a grave.

CHAPTER 26

The hand wrapped itself around my ankle. I opened my mouth to scream, but nothing came out. This was like a nightmare, except no nightmare had ever been this vivid, this real, this squelchy and cold.

The ground beneath me shifted and another hand poked through, grubby fingers scrabbling for purchase against the dirt.

I yanked my ankle away just as the creature dragged itself fully out of the grave. A graveyard ghoul! Another hand poked out of the dirt.

There were more of them. And they were all coming up from beneath the ground, coming for us.

Hannah and I crisscrossed through the gravestones, Champ and Stine on our heels, ducking past tombs and beneath statues. The muddy ghouls lumbered after us, more of them clawing up from the dirt all around. I tried not to think about what would happen if they caught up, those pale faces, those dirt-caked hands, dragging us down deep, under the ground, into the grave . . .

Finally, we reached the gate of the cemetery. Hannah slipped through the wrought-iron rungs pretty easily. It was a tighter squeeze for me, but I made it.

Champ and Stine were almost to safety—when a ghoul grabbed Stine's foot.

"Save yourselves!" he cried as the ghoul yanked hard, dragging him back into the graveyard. "Hey—dumbhead! I didn't mean it!" Stine shouted angrily.

Hannah and I spun around. We dove beside him. We each took an arm and pulled as hard as we could.

It was like human tug-of-war. Inch by inch, we pulled him toward our side of the gate. But the ghouls wouldn't let go. Stine looked like he was about to be split in two.

There were more ghouls tugging on Stine now, all of them pulling in sync. And they were stronger than we were. My fingers were going numb, and I could see Hannah's hands starting to slip. We were losing him!

"What! Kind! Of! Monster!" Stine shouted with rage. He kicked ghouls in the face with each word. It startled them, and their grip loosened—just for a second. But that second was enough for Hannah and me to pull Stine out of their grasp and through the gate.

We both collapsed into the dirt, wheezing loudly, struggling to breathe. I felt as if my arms were going to fall off.

Stine was already on his feet, scanning the parking lot for Champ. "I want to have a little talk with that kid. Where

is that little goofball?"

Champ peeked out from behind a bush, closer than I'd thought. "I'm so sorry, sir. You told me to run, so I felt that that's what you wanted me to do. In your heart."

Stine gave him a hard stare. "Not your fault," he said finally. "I'm the one who wrote those ghouls. Maybe next time I'll write about cute little minnows swimming sweetly in a pond."

He sighed. "Forget I said that. They'd only turn into man-eating sharks."

"Maybe those are the last of your monsters we'll have to fight," I said.

Of course, I was wrong.

CHAPTER 27

In the Madison High gym, a few students danced, gyrating on the dance floor. Some drank punch, awkwardly standing around in the corner waiting for someone of the opposite sex to acknowledge their existence. It was your average, everyday school dance.

But over on our side of the school, the building was dark and empty, hibernating until Monday morning. It felt totally wrong to be there when we didn't have to be. Like a violation of some law of nature—Thou Shalt Never Go to School Unless Absolutely Necessary.

On the other hand, this was pretty necessary. Somewhere in the enormous maze of lobby display cases, Stine's typewriter was waiting.

"I thought it was down here," Stine said, after we'd hit the end of the third corridor. "Or is it that way? Maybe we should split up."

Champ groaned. "Do you not read your own horror books? You *never* split up."

"He's right. Let's go," Hannah said. "We need to get that

typewriter."

We found it in the last place we expected—tucked into a display case outside the gym. Music from inside the gym thumped in the background, and my heart beat in time. My mom was so close by, but I couldn't worry about that now. I just had to trust that she was okay. No one inside the gym was screaming, which was a good sign.

Stine grinned at the sight of his typewriter—then scowled when he realized what was sharing space with it in the case.

"They put Stephen King's fountain pen front and center!" he whined, rapping on the glass so hard that the STEPHEN KING'S PEN placard trembled.

"Yeah, that seems like the right thing to focus on." I examined the lock holding the case closed. "I need to find a paper clip."

Stine shook his head. "There's no time. I'm going to break the glass. I need a trash can or—"

"Or that," I said as Hannah just slid the case open. I guess security was pretty lax at this school.

Stine grabbed the typewriter, hugging it to his chest. "I've missed you so much, darling."

We didn't have time for this. I got the feeling we didn't have much time for anything. "All right. So start writing. Did you remember we're in some kind of a hurry?"

He looked up at me, still clutching the typewriter.

"What's the plot?"

What else? "Monsters lose. Good guys win. The end!"

"No," he said, annoyed. "It doesn't work unless it's a real Goosebumps story: twists and turns and frights and surprises."

I don't know about everyone else. But to me, that seemed like a whole lot to come up with in the next ten minutes.

"Go to the gym. Warn everyone," Stine told us. He'd started shuffling toward the auditorium. "Get them to barricade the school."

"And where are you going?" Hannah asked.

"To find a place to write. Buy me as much time as you can. Slappy's going to come for me. I have a deadline—literally."

We all groaned.

He started down the hall. "Let's go!"

We went. When I looked back, Stine was slamming Stephen King's pen against the wall, trying to break it. When that didn't work, he hurled it into a water fountain.

Nothing to worry about, I told myself, trying my best to believe it. *This guy can totally save the world.*

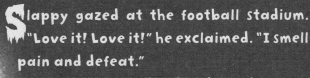

Slappy gazed at the football stadium. "Love it! Love it!" he exclaimed. "I smell pain and defeat."

He sat on the hood of his car,

surrounded by his most trusted buddies. The werewolf. The vampire poodles. The snowman. The bug-eyed aliens. The gray-faced, dirt-encrusted graveyard ghouls. They awaited his orders. They trusted him. They would do anything for him. Because they owed him their freedom.

They knew he would do anything to keep them free—forever.

Slappy swayed along with the melody trickling from the car radio. It was a glorious night. If he listened hard, he could hear terrified shrieks floating on the breeze.

The helpful gnomes unloaded a trunkful of manuscripts onto the fifty-yard line. Slappy offered them the key, and they began the noble work. One by one, they turned the locks on every manuscript.

"Not that one," Slappy suddenly called. "Not just yet."

That one he was saving for something special.

"Now," Slappy said, and the gnomes opened the book covers. Monster after monster climbed off the pages, roaring and bellowing and screeching with rage. They'd been locked up a long time.

They were hungry.

"All my Facebook friends together in one place." Slappy laughed. "I do crack myself up. Now it's time to crack up some other people."

He tossed a match onto the pile of books, and they instantly burst into flames.

There was no going back.

CHAPTER 28

"So, this is what a high school dance is like?" Hannah said.

I looked around.

Girls parading in their hippest outfits while guys stared at their phones, pretending to ignore them? Check.

Excruciatingly awkward first dates? Check.

Angry teacher dragging lame guy away by his earlobe? Check.

Two wannabes rocking out in the middle of the dance floor and no one paying any attention? Double-check.

"Yeah," I told her. "Usually the dancing's better."

It was all pretty standard and pretty lame, but Hannah was gaping around her like she was in a foreign country. And I guess, for her, that's what high school was. Had she really spent her entire life locked up in the house, only sneaking out at night? What kind of life was that?

Just then, I heard an extremely familiar voice screaming my name.

"Mom!" I called. I caught sight of her pushing through the crowd toward me.

She wrapped me in a giant bear hug. Normally, that was one hundred percent against my pretend-we-don't-know-each-other-while-on-school-grounds rule. But this time, I just hugged her back, wishing I could hold on forever.

"I couldn't reach you or Aunt Lorraine!" she exclaimed. "I was worried about you!"

I hadn't realized until now how worried I'd been about her, too. But there wasn't time to explain all that, much less calm down her inevitable freak-out if she heard what I'd been doing all night.

"Mom, everyone here is in danger," I told her. "We have to barricade the school."

Her face fell. "Zach, come on. Not this again."

I couldn't believe she thought I'd make something like this up.

"He's telling the truth," Hannah said, then held out her hand. "Hi, I'm Hannah. I live next door."

While my mom was distracted trying to figure out what I was doing at a school dance with a *girl*, Champ and I jumped up onstage.

Champ bumped the DJ out of the way and grabbed the mic, talking over everyone's loud groans. "Everyone! Everyone! Eyes up here! Listen up, I have something to say!"

Hundreds of pairs of eyes turned toward him, waiting for something momentous.

"Er . . . everyone, listen to my best friend, Zach!"

He shoved the mic at me.

"Okay, this is going to sound insane, but monsters have invaded Madison," I began. "They've blocked every road out of town, and they've torn down all the cell towers. We've been cut off from the rest of the world. They're outside the school right now. We need to work to—"

Someone in the back let out a thunderous belch.

As the room exploded into laughter, I suddenly had a lot of sympathy for my mom, and vice principals everywhere.

A jock started screaming, pointing over his shoulder at the window that looked out over the stadium. "He's right! It's the boogeyman . . . and he's picking his nose!"

I wondered if I could convince Stine to write a book about the Boogeyman Who Ate Jocks for Dessert.

Over the heads of the crowd, I could see the guy's smug face and the high fives he gave all his grinning friends as the whole student body laughed in my face.

Then I saw him turn and actually *look* out the window.

He screamed again. "There's a giant bug, and it's eating everyone's cars!"

Another jock gave him the cut-it-out signal. "Dude, it's getting old."

"No, seriously—" But before he could finish, a gigantic praying mantis pincer crashed through the window and yanked him straight through.

No one laughed. The gym fell totally silent as a towering

bug eye peered through the broken glass at us.

The silence lasted about three more seconds. And then?

Then the entire gym, hundreds of students and chaperones alike, went out of their minds. Screaming, shouting, crying, gnashing teeth, begging for mommy and daddy to come and save them, shouting for the cops, calling for help, calling for *anyone oh my god someone help us.*

It was deafening chaos, and it wasn't going to help anyone.

"Everyone calm down," I screamed. "I know what to do. But I can't do it myself."

Silence rippled over the crowd again, and they looked at me like they *believed* me—like I had all the answers and could actually save the day.

At which point I kind of freaked out, myself. Because who was I to save anything?

Hannah must have seen the panic in my eyes. She gave me one of her best smiles, the kind that said *You can do it. I know you can.*

And that was all it took for me to know it, too.

"Look, those things out there, they're R.L. Stine's monsters. He's here. He can fix this. But we need to buy him time to write. So . . . who here has read Goosebumps?"

No one moved. Up onstage, Champ raised his hand proudly. One by one, the kids in the audience followed him, until almost everyone in the gym had their hands in the air.

"Good. Then you'll all know what to do."

CHAPTER 29

It felt kind of weird to be in charge.

But also kind of awesome.

The first order of business was finding as many things as possible that could work as weapons: mops and buckets from the janitor's closet, bats, golf clubs, hockey sticks, and tennis rackets from the equipment closet.

Then I sent the principal and a group of students out to drag some desks from the classrooms and stack them in front of the gym, so we'd have a barricade against the monsters if they came at us.

We didn't have to wait long for the attack. A crew of tiny, red-eyed robots powered through the barricades, shooting lasers out of their eyes. I recognized them: Annihilator 3000s, determined to annihilate *us*.

Twelve-foot-tall scarecrows punched straw fists through the windows onto the courtyard. I sent a bunch of kids and teachers up to the roof with baseball bats and balls to try to knock the stuffing out of them.

The rest of us evacuated to the cafeteria and barricaded

ourselves behind some overturned tables—just before the vampires attacked.

Fortunately, we had the perfect weapons: serving spoons and a vat of garlic mashed potatoes.

"You sure this will work?" Champ asked.

I scooped up a giant chunk of mush. "Vampires hate garlic, right?"

"Yeah . . . but do they hate garlic mashed potatoes?"

A vampire and his vampire bride were closing in. Not far behind them, their vampire poodle levitated toward us.

Hannah scooped up a spoonful of potatoes. "Let's find out, already!"

"Fire!" I shouted, and we let loose with a barrage of garlic mashed potatoes. The vampires screeched in pain and fled. "I can't believe that actually—"

Another vampire peeked his head into the gym, and we hit him with everything we had left.

Instead of fleeing, the vampire wiped all the potato gunk off his face. "Guys, it's just me," he said quietly.

I recognized that face: It was the Goth kid who sat behind me in chemistry.

"Uh, sorry, Seth," Champ said.

There was no time for apologies. We had lawn gnomes to explode with bowling balls. Bug-eyed aliens to melt with Bunsen burners! A mummy to unravel with an Elmer's-glue trap! Mutant insects to swat with baseball bats!

"Only a little longer," I called to Hannah as we blasted through two more giant bug heads. "Stine should almost be done!"

I just hoped that wasn't wishful thinking.

The author sat at a large wooden desk in the center of a dark stage, staring at his typewriter.

"The night was dark," he mumbled to himself, punching at the keys halfheartedly. But . . . no.

"Dark was the night."

Better.

"The darkness embraced the night."

Then he had it. He rested his hands over the keys.

"The night was cold."

A cool breeze kissed the back of his neck. He looked up, suddenly on alert.

Not that it would save him.

Slappy paced the hallways, closing in. "Papa, where are you?" he called. "I want to see your face. I haven't had a good laugh all night."

Stine tried to ignore the sense that the darkness was enveloping him. He typed furiously, faster and faster.

"All the monsters had converged. The vicious vampire bats, the praying mantis, the haunted mask—"

"Forgetting somebody?" a tinny voice interrupted.

Stine looked up. The auditorium was dark. Only a single spotlight lit Stine's desk onstage, and in its glare, he could see nothing. But he knew the dummy was there.

"Slappy?"

Giggles echoed through the empty room. Another spotlight flared, revealing Slappy in a seat in the middle of the audience.

He smiled at his creator. "Good to see you up on the stage," the dummy cackled. "Are you ready for your final curtain?"

"How did you find me?" Stine demanded.

"I smelled you. Or was that something I stepped in on the sidewalk?" Slappy cackled at his bad joke. "You can't hide from me. Because I know you. I created you. Or is it the other way around?" He giggled. "I always forget. We're so much alike . . ."

The light went out. Slappy disappeared.

"Slappy?" Stine called, panic in his voice. "Where are you?"

Lights on: Slappy was closer now, sitting in the front row. "Think you look good up there?" he rasped. "I've seen better heads on a cabbage!"

"What do you want?" Stine demanded.

"I've decided to give you a choice. Work with me, and you can live. Work against me, and . . ." He giggled. How he loved the sound of his own evil laughter. "Well, you'll miss all the fun."

"No, Slappy. I don't want that."

Slappy stared at Stine and said, "I know you better than you know yourself. 'I'm done,' you say. 'I'll never write again.' But you always come back to me. Because you need me. Because you *are* me."

Stine grimaced. "We are not the—"

"—same person?" Slappy said the words along with him. Then he laughed. "See? I know your every thought—your deepest, darkest fantasies, Papa. You made me this way. We share everything."

Stine stood, shouting, "No! Things have changed."

Slappy shook his head. "Changed? The only thing you should change is your underwear!"

The auditorium went totally dark.

"Slappy?" Stine called. "Slappy?"

But Stine should have known better than to make Slappy unhappy. When the stage lights came on again, Slappy was standing on the desk, holding Stine's new pages.

Slappy read: "'Everyone in the high school joined forces to defeat Slappy and his monsters.'"

No, that wouldn't do.

Slappy improvised his own line. "'But Slappy had other ideas.'"

Stine reached for the pages; Slappy reached for Stine. He grabbed the writer's fingers and pulled back hard.

There was a sickening crunch, then a gasp of pain.

"Oops. Did that hurt?" Slappy giggled. "My bad! Ha-ha-ha."

Bad wasn't the word for it. The author wouldn't be writing anything more. Not tonight.

CHAPTER 30

Hannah and I could hear Stine groaning in pain from outside the auditorium. We burst through the doors.

He was alone onstage, sitting by his typewriter, holding his hand tenderly, as if it were an injured bird.

"That evil dummy broke my fingers!" he shouted.

Hannah rushed over to help her father.

"I only had a page or two more," he sighed.

"Forget two pages," I suggested. "Just write two words: *The End.*"

He shook his head. "That's not how it works."

Suddenly, the building started to shake. Something told me it wasn't an earthquake.

The PA system buzzed, and the principal's voice boomed. "I have an emergency announcement! Monsters have overwhelmed Madison High. Retreat to the storage room in an orderly fashion."

I grabbed the pages and the typewriter. "We'll figure this out later. Just run!"

We raced down the hallway, dodging monsters every

few feet. The principal was right, they were everywhere—man-eating plants blasting out of lockers, bug-eyed aliens marching in lockstep with their freeze rays on full blast, scarecrows, not to mention a jack-o'-lantern creature, bog monster, scary clown, and witch doctor. All of them were chasing us—but somehow we made it through the doors and into the night.

We crossed the quad and made it into the gym storage room, closing ourselves in with the rest of the student body. Champ and I barricaded the entrance.

Zombies and scarecrows pressed their faces to the window, banging on the glass. The ceiling quaked. Plaster dropped in drifts and clumps. Something was up there, determined to get in.

Roars echoed beyond the barricade. Maybe we were safe for now, but not for long.

"What now?" Champ asked. "They're gonna get in here."

"I don't know," I admitted.

Stine gestured at the window facing the parking lot. Most of the cars were crushed, but a row of school buses was lined up and ready to go.

"Slappy wants me," Stine said. "That's who he's after. If I can lead the monsters away on one of those buses, I know they'll follow me—and you'll all be safe."

Hannah looked horrified. "Then I'm coming with you!"

"Hannah, no." Stine rested a hand on her shoulder. "I've

run away from people my whole life. I was so mad at the real world that I created these terrible monsters. But I'm not mad anymore. This is my fault. I made this. Not this town. Not you."

Hannah shook her head. I wondered if she'd even heard him. "There's got to be another way!"

"Sweetheart, it's time for me to face my demons."

Champ held out his hand for a fist bump. "I believe in you."

"Shut up," Stine said. Then he took a deep breath and reconsidered. "I'm sorry. I mean, thank you for believing in me."

I couldn't believe it. Maybe people really could change, even people like Stine. Were we really going to let him go out there on his own, into the jaws of certain death?

Then I noticed a tackling dummy tucked into the back corner of the room.

And I had an idea.

Slappy watched the author sneak onto the bus. He listened to the roar of the engine. He watched the bus pull away from the gym.

"Oh, Papa, where are you going?"

Slappy crooned. "I thought we could watch the destruction together. I got us the best seats in the house." He flipped a hand at his army of monsters. "Bring him to me."

Then he thought about it for a moment.

"Actually, just KILL him. I'm getting bored with this game."

The order had been given.

The monsters galloped and stomped and lumbered after the bus. Slappy followed them in his car, laughing from all the excitement. Very soon, it would be over. Very soon, the author would die. But his creations would live on. And Slappy would lead them all. "I'm writing the story from now on! And trust me, it's a horror story!"

The bus hurtled down the dark highway, blazing a path through the night. Then, a flicker of giant wings cut through the darkness. A loud hissing sliced through the silence.

The giant praying mantis descended on the bus, kicking it down the highway. The bus rolled and rolled before coming to a stop, its roof nearly torn off, its metal crushed and scorched from road burn.

Inside the wreck, there was nothing but silence.

The monsters crept toward the twisted metal ruin, eager to see the lifeless body that lay inside.

Closer . . . closer . . . until they were close enough to

discover that the lifeless body was a tackling dummy dressed in the author's coat.

A hockey stick was propped against the gas pedal. A leather belt bound the wheel in place.

The monsters roared in anger.

One of the ghouls found a wire lining the side of the door. It tugged once, twice, and then there was a strange clicking sound.

The bus exploded.

CHAPTER 31

"It worked!" I crowed, peering through the window of our bus as we sped past the explosion. *Who knew that paying attention in chemistry would pay off in such a satisfying way?*

"Woo-hoo!" Hannah cheered.

Even Stine cracked a smile. "Okay, now, where were we?" He was dictating as he drove. I typed.

"'Stine's ingenious plan worked to perfection,'" he said.

I stopped typing. *Stine's* ingenious plan?

"Am I going too fast?" he said. "'Stine's bravery was beyond measure. He had blown the monsters to bits and single-handedly saved an entire town. He was an American hero, but he didn't need to brag about it because that wasn't his style.'"

"You want me to write that last line?" I asked. *This* guy had sold four hundred million copies worldwide?

"I'm the writer!" he insisted. "You're the secretary! Just write what I say."

"Where are we going?" Champ asked.

"Slappy will know wherever I go," Stine said. "Because

he is me." He didn't seem very happy about it. "We have to go somewhere I've never been. Somewhere I don't even know exists."

"I know where to go," Hannah said.

I was pretty sure I knew where she meant.

◇ ◇ ◇

The abandoned amusement park looked even creepier now that I knew that monsters were real. But Hannah was right, this was the perfect spot. It would buy us the time we needed.

The four of us scrambled out of the bus and hurried across the park.

"'It was clear that there was only one place in the park left to hide,'" Stine dictated.

"I can't type while I'm running," I pointed out.

"Just . . . mental note. 'There was only one place in the park left to hide. The . . . arcade gallery!'"

"Uh, there is no arcade gallery," Hannah said.

Stine craned his neck around. "'That was, in fact, a fun house!'" he corrected himself.

The fun house was a maze of mirrors. We crept through a kaleidoscope of distorted reflections, our faces grotesquely stretched out and squeezed in.

Hannah shined the flashlight at the keys so I could see

what I was doing. I typed as fast as I could.

"'The fun house was terrifying,'" Stine intoned. "'Not so much for Stine as for the others, of course. But it offered refuge from the real monsters that lurked outside.'"

Speaking of real monsters . . .

"Well, here you are in a fun house," a familiar voice rasped. "And guess what? The fun is just beginning!"

Slappy had found us.

CHAPTER 32

All the fun house lights flashed red. Slappy stood before a huge mirror. Half his face was burned and charred from the bus explosion. He looked angrier than ever.

"Papa, you left without saying good-bye," he said.

Slappy and Stine faced off before the mirror, their grotesque reflections strangely identical.

"I was a good friend and you turned your back on me, locked me up, imprisoned me in the pages of a book. You stuck me on a shelf for years and years. The key was right there, and you never used it."

"You're not real, Slappy," Stine said. "I created you, and I can write you out."

Slappy laughed. "I'm writing the story now. So sorry there's no part for a character named Stine."

Slappy held up a manuscript. "Let's introduce a new character. Maybe the Blob That Ate Everyone?"

Stine's face lost all its color. "No, no, not him, Slappy."

"He just wants to say hi, maybe have a quick bite. Ha-ha-ha."

He pulled out the golden key and unlocked the book. Then . . .

"Run!" Stine shouted.

A gelatinous mass burst out of the pages. It oozed through the rotted walls and floor, spreading rapidly, making hungry swallowing sounds, heading straight for us.

The four of us ran out of the fun house—and right into the path of what remained of the monster army. We were cut off.

"The Ferris wheel!" Hannah shouted, and we ran for it. Stine pressed the unfinished manuscript into my hands.

"Go," he said. "I'll hold them off. Finish the book."

"Wait, what do I write? What's the end?"

"Zach." Stine moved closer to me as he spoke. "I realize now that the reason Hannah connected with you is because there's something in you that's like me. You can do this, Zach. End it."

Could I do it? Could I end it?

I guessed I didn't have much choice. Stine ran off before Hannah could stop him.

Champ, Hannah, and I climbed up the rusty spokes of the Ferris wheel, making it to the top just as Stine reached the Blob That Ate Everyone.

The Blob swallowed Stine whole. Then its whole ghastly body shivered and quaked in an enormous burp.

Hannah screamed for her father, her voice exploding

with pain. She tried to climb down toward him, but Champ and I held her in place.

It killed me to hear her in so much pain, but I couldn't let her sacrifice herself. Not when it was already too late to save her father.

"Wait, look!" Champ exclaimed. He pointed at the Blob—a Stine-shaped figure was punching from the inside. "He's still alive in there!"

From our perch on the Ferris wheel, we spotted Slappy walking toward the Blob. There was nothing we could do but watch.

"Hey, Blob-food! You're trapped," the dummy taunted Stine. "That's what it felt like to be locked inside your books. Not so much fun, is it?"

I was supposed to be writing, but the scene was so grotesque and wrong, I couldn't tear my eyes away. Until I noticed movement at the bottom of the Ferris wheel. The monster army had reached it—and they were *climbing* it.

"They're coming!" Champ squeaked. "What are we gonna do?"

"Buy us some time!" Hannah ordered him.

Champ bent toward the ground. "Get out of here!" he shouted at the monsters. Then he turned back to Hannah. "That didn't do anything."

Champ took off his shoe and hurled it at the closest ghoul. The ghoul kept climbing. "That didn't do anything, either."

Okay. I had to try to finish the story. I didn't know if what I was typing made any sense, or if it would work, but I just kept typing. I had to. Stine had left it up to me.

"Can you write faster?" Champ urged me.

"It's really hard without a mouse!" I complained.

But that wasn't the problem. The problem was finding the right words. Stine was right—this storytelling stuff was harder than it looked.

"Finish it, Zach," Hannah murmured.

I knew she was counting on me. They all were.

I took a deep breath, and then I finished it:

"'As the monsters converged, Zach closed his eyes, opened the book, and the monsters were swallowed back into the world of paper and ink, NEVER TO BE SEEN AGAIN. THE END!'"

I yanked the last page out of the typewriter.

"What happens now?" Champ asked.

The praying mantis was gnawing on the Ferris wheel bolts. Any longer and the monsters wouldn't need to come up here to get us—because we'd all collapse down to the ground in a deadly heap.

"We're about to find out," I said.

I shuffled the pages together and put them inside Stine's leather manuscript cover, then closed the book.

"It'll work," Hannah said. "I know it."

The mantis chomped one last bolt, and there was a terrifying scream of metal. The Ferris wheel rolled right off its base.

"Hang on!" I cried, grabbing tight to the closest rung as we started spinning out of control.

The Ferris wheel car spun round and round . . . and the manuscript flew out of my hands!

CHAPTER 33

"Grab it!" I shouted, reaching desperately.

The Ferris wheel tipped over on its side and smashed to the ground like a gigantic quarter. We all tumbled onto the ground, somehow miraculously in one piece, but . . .

"The manuscript!" I looked around, but couldn't see it anywhere. "Do you have it?"

We'd rolled far enough that we were safe for the moment, but the monsters would be coming for us, and fast.

Hannah shook her head.

There was a groan from inside the Ferris wheel car. Champ crawled out, looking wobbly but triumphant. He raised the manuscript in the air. "Caught it."

I grabbed the book. All I had to do was open it, and all the monsters would be sucked inside.

All the monsters. It suddenly hit me, what that meant.

I froze.

"Come on! What are you waiting for?" Champ said. "Open the book! All the monsters will be here any second!"

"Open the book, Scaredy-Cat!" Hannah cried.

I opened the book.

The tornado was stronger than before. It was like a black hole, sucking in every monster in sight.

Whoosh . . . whoosh . . . whoosh . . . scarecrows, werewolves, gargoyles, gnomes, all of them flying through the air past us, sucked and swirled into the vortex of the book.

The force knocked the book out of my hands. It landed on the ground, just in time for the humongous blob to be pulled in and sucked away from Stine.

Slappy leaped onto him, wrapping his little arms around Stine's neck, and together they hurtled toward us. Slappy was powerless against the force of the book.

"I don't like this!" Slappy screamed. "The weather forecast didn't call for a tornado! Slappy isn't happy!"

"Neither is Stine!" Stine roared, struggling to peel Slappy away with all his might. "Stupid dummy!" he shouted, giving Slappy a vicious kick that sent him straight into the heart of the vortex.

Slappy clawed at the dirt, trying to hold on. But Stine stepped down hard on his fingers. I heard a loud *craaack*.

"Now we're even," Stine said.

The dummy swirled into the furious wind, shrieking as he disappeared back into the swirling void. "See you in your

dreams!" he called just before he vanished.

Champ slammed the book shut, and the wind went still.

"I did it!" he shouted, pumping his fists in the air. "I saved us!"

I looked at Stine and shrugged. He just grinned at me.

So did Hannah.

CHAPTER 34

They rebuilt the town. Fortunately, there wasn't all that much of it in the first place, so it didn't take too long.

Pretty soon, everyone had managed to forget about the night the monsters invaded, or at least they pretended to. I guess it was easier for them to think they'd imagined it than to believe that monsters existed, that they could come back.

They didn't realize that some things never come back.

The school closed for a couple weeks so they could repair the damage. Champ and Hannah came over a lot to watch TV and play video games. Champ was always coming up with some excuse to get out of his house. Down in his basement he had a copy of every Goosebumps book ever written, and he told me that sometimes, in the middle of the night, he was pretty sure he heard the characters talking to one another.

But that was just Champ being Champ. Probably.

I found stuff to do. I hung around with my mom sometimes. And I saw a lot of Stine, who'd started going out with Aunt Lorraine.

Hannah and I spent as much time together as we could.

We went on long walks at night, always avoiding the grave-yard and the amusement park. One evening we even checked out Sushi Wednesday. It wasn't as bad as I thought it'd be.

Finally, the school opened its doors again. I was almost glad to go back. It was weird, though, driving over there with my mom, almost exactly as we had on my first day. How could everything feel the same when so much horror had happened here?

Mom pulled into her parking space. "Okay, I'll give you a sixty-second head start," she said, winking.

Maybe not everything felt the same. "It's okay, Mom. Let's go in together."

She grinned at me. Then, as I went to open the door, she locked it before I could.

"So immature," I teased, but it was good to know some things would never change.

◇　◇　◇

School was different.

Really different.

I'm talking *Invasion of the Body Snatchers* different.

Suddenly, I was the most popular kid in the building. Everyone knew my name, everyone wanted to say hi to me and be my friend, or act like it. Apparently, when you help save the student body from being eaten by an army of mon-

sters, it makes you kind of popular.

I followed Champ into English class. It was a big day for us—not just the first day back at school, but the first day with a new teacher.

The classroom buzzed with speculation, everyone offering guesses for who our sub would be.

I just sat back in my chair and listened. I couldn't wait to see their faces when they found out.

Mr. Boyd's replacement stepped into the room. His hair was neatly slicked back, his glasses pushed up high on his nose.

"Hello, my name is Mr. R.L. Stine, and I will be your new English teacher. It seems Mr. Boyd is still recovering from injuries sustained by a mutant insect."

Stine didn't even wait for a reaction before turning to the board and starting his lesson.

"Now, every story ever told can be broken up into three distinct parts: the beginning, the middle, and . . . *the twist.*"

◊   ◊   ◊

I'd had enough twists. I was looking forward to a nice, long, boring, uneventful year. Or maybe life. I figured I'd had my adventure, I'd gotten to be a hero, and now there was nothing left to do but my homework. And hurry home to see Hannah.

"Um, now that you're teaching here, do you ever think

about letting Hannah come to school?" I asked Stine as we walked toward the parking lot after school. He'd offered to give me a ride home. "After all, your secret's kind of out of the bag."

"Not a day goes by I don't consider it," he said. "And today's the day I finally realized something." He paused for a minute. "I can't keep her locked away forever like my manuscripts."

I was puzzled for a minute. Then Stine pointed down the hall. There was Hannah! She was carrying a backpack, just like any other Madison High student. And she was heading our way.

"Hannah!" I hurried toward her.

"Easy with the hands!" Stine called after us.

I waved at him, and then took Hannah's hand in mine. "So, now that you're the new kid in school, can I give you a tour? No monsters this time around, I promise."

Hannah smiled up at me. "I'd love that."

Before he left the school building that day, the author decided to visit his old typewriter. It was back in its display case, and this time there was no Stephen King pen next to it, competing for kids' attention.

He looked fondly at the old machine, thinking of all the good times they'd had together.

Not to mention all the horrifying, terrifying, hair-raising times . . . but wasn't that kind of the same thing?

Maybe, someday, he could risk writing something again. Nothing too terrible, of course. Nothing with a carnivorous rhododendron or a seven-story guinea pig, but a story. It would be so satisfying to get his fingers on the keys again (once they'd healed, at least). It would be like scratching an itch.

He was thinking so hard about typing that when one of the keys started to move, he assumed he was imagining it.

But no: The *I* key was trembling. Then, with a sharp clack, it snapped down, as if pressed by an invisible finger.

Stine's breath caught in his throat.

The *N* key clicked down next. Then the *V*.

No, Stine thought. *Please, no. It can't be.*

The typewriter didn't listen to him. Someone else was in control now. One impossible key at a time, it spelled out:

THE INVISIBLE BOY'S REVENGE

Stine could see his horrified reflection in the glass. And beside it, he saw something else. A greasy child-sized handprint.

It was time to play.

The Original Bone-Chilling Series